MW00570122

Goat-Song

and Other Stories

David Ross

En Route Books and Media, LLC

Saint Louis, MO

En Route Books and Media, LLC

5705 Rhodes Avenue

St. Louis, MO 63109

Contact us at contactus@enroutebooksandmedia.com

Cover credit: Sebastian Mahfood with images from
Hieronymous Bosch (circa 1450-1516); The Last Judgment (after
1482) and The Garden of Earthly Delights (bet. 1490 and 1510)
© 2022 David Ross

ISBN-13: 978-1-956715-71-2

Library of Congress Control Number: 2022941972

All rights reserved. No part of this book may be reproduced,
stored in a retrieval system, or transmitted in any form, or by any
means, electronic, mechanical, photocopying, or otherwise, without the prior written permission of the author.

Table of Contents

Goat-Song 1

Gaps 123

Poison 149

Goat-Song

Prologue

The door opens behind me, and I hear footsteps approaching. My vision is cut off from warm hands covering my eyes. "Are you ready?" a voice asks. The voice is digitally modified.

I spin in my chair, and there is my Sarah, laughing. "Are you ready, Dad?" she asks, speaking normally, the voice modifier lowered.

"Almost," I say. "I need to finish this article. I'll be right out."

Faith enters the room with a cup of coffee. She sets it on my desk. "It's ten-thirty," she says, "we're ready when you are." Faith nudges the coffee toward me as if it were an elixir, a liquid answer, though I'm not sure what the question is.

"I'm almost finished," I say. I grab the mug and drink. "I'll be right out. If you and Sarah pack the truck, we'll be able to leave sooner."

While I'm finishing the article, I hear them packing. Ice thuds into the cooler, the rubber of the refrigerator door smacks as it opens and closes, the front door opens, and the screen door swishes as they load the truck.

I skim through the article for the last time and then send it to my editor. I drink the last of the coffee and walk into the kitchen. Faith and Sarah are sitting at the table, looking at their phones. "Are you ready?" I ask.

They both hold up one finger to me while typing on their phones and I cannot tell if they are mocking me or not. Faith finishes first, puts her phone in her purse and stands. Sarah stands while finishing the last of her message. She slides the phone into her pocket, looks at me and smiles. They both walk out the front door. I lock the door and walk to the truck. I check the hitch to make sure the trailer is secured, and I check the boat to make sure it is secured to the trailer. I get into the driver's seat.

Sarah is in the truck, but Faith is standing in the street to help me back out of the driveway. "Who were you texting?" I ask Sarah as I look in the rearview mirror. Faith is waiving me out.

"No one," she says.

"No one? When I meet this No One, what will he look like?"

"He? What makes you think it's a boy?"

"You can either explain the ontology of nothingness and how you're texting a Nothing, or you can admit that you're texting a Someone, who's probably a boy."

"It's not a boy," she says, "and it's not a Nothing. It's Hannah."

"Which one's Hannah?"

"The one you call Frumpy."

"I thought that was Emily."

"No, Emily's Spaghetti-Moe."

"Oh yes. You don't tell them I call them those things, right?"

"Why, you scared of teenage girls?"

"I don't want to pay their psychiatric bills."

Faith motions for me to stop. She walks to the truck and gets in. "OK," says Faith, "let's go."

#

There are already visitors to the lake but there is not a large crowd. I back the boat onto the dock while Faith stands in the water, guiding the boat. "Why don't you help your mother?" I half ask, half command of Sarah. She smiles and quickly gets out of the truck. This is her first time launching, and for her the novelty has not yet developed into a chore.

In the mirror, I see Faith talking to Sarah, pointing to different areas of the boat and the trailer, showing her what to watch for and how to unhook the boat from the trailer. Faith waves at me and motions for me to continue lowering the boat down the dock and into the water. She says something to Sarah, and Sarah puts up her hand for me to stop. They walk around the boat, unhooking the straps and disconnecting the boat from the trailer and the truck. They get into the boat and wave at me to launch them. I reverse into the water until they drift from the trailer.

I drive the trailer out of the water, put the truck in park and step out. "We'll be near the big rock," shouts Faith from the boat. I nod. Faith starts the engine and steers the boat into the lake.

I get into the truck and drive to the parking lot. My phone vibrates. It's a text from Sarah:

We're at the rock.

I close the message app and there is an unread email. It's from my editor:

Received the article. Looks good. Enjoy your weekend and see you Monday. Beth.

A car parks next to me. A man steps out of it. He is small and pale with sunglasses and a cap. He looks at me and smiles. I smile back and exit the truck.

"Beautiful day," he says. "Let's hope it stays this way."

"I don't think the forecast predicted any change," I say.

He does not respond to this. He is confused for a moment, but then smiles again. "You'll forgive me," he says, "I was lost in thought."

"That's all right."

"Are you here with family?" I detect a hint of an accent, maybe Swiss.

"Yes. Are you?"

He shakes his head. "I'm here for work."

"What do you do?"

"I'm a quantum physicist."

"What does a quantum physicist want with the lake?" I ask.

He smiles. "It's complicated. But have you noticed anything strange around here?"

"Strange how?"

"Never mind. You'd know it if you saw it."

The man looks disappointed. He sighs and looks around, lost in his search. Then he stops and gives a muffled cry. "Like that," he says, pointing across the river.

Across the river there is a single tree that is—I don't know—it looks like it's flickering, like a glitch in computer software. It is only for a moment and then it stops. The tree is far enough away that it seems more like an illusion than anything else.

But the man is giddy, writing in a small notebook. "Thank you," he says, and he blows a kiss toward the tree. He turns toward his car and almost runs into me, forgetting about me already. "Oh," he says, "excuse me. Please, enjoy the day with your family." He gets into his car and drives away.

As I watch the man drive away, there is a cry for help. Quickly, I try to find the direction of the cry, and I see a crowd gathering along the shore. They are gathering near the big rock.

At first, I walk quickly, then I jog, then I run toward the shore as it dawns on me by degrees that the crowd is gathering in the vicinity of my boat and that my boat is beached and damaged. I hear the cry for help again. It is Faith calling for help, standing in the boat above the crowd. She sees me along the shore, and she points to the middle of the lake so that I do not run to her but run to something else. People are gathering around her, thinking that she is in need of assistance, but she is pointing to the water, trying to draw the crowd's attention away from her. In the middle of the lake, I see Sarah surface and buoy. I remove my shoes and my shirt, and I rush into the lake, swimming to her. The world shuts out, and I cannot hear anything except the splashes of water and the whimpers of Sarah. I swim frantically and swallow water. As I come close to her, she submerges, and I take a breath and follow her under. I cannot see in the lake water. My eyes sting, and I struggle to keep them open. I guess where she might be and swim toward her. Something brushes against my leg, and I quickly reposition, darting my hand toward the thing against my leg, and I grab her hand. She squeezes my hand, but I feel her squeeze loosen and then she slips away from me. I am almost out of oxygen, but I try to swim toward her though I cannot feel her. Something latches onto my back and pulls me to the surface. A rescuer lifts me out of the water. When I surface, I gasp for air and I say, "No, she's right there, she's right there," and multiple rescuers dive in the direction I'm pointing, but the one who pulled me out of the water will not let me go. "She's right there," I say, defeated, and I still feel the sensation of her hand on my hand, and I see, on the other side of the lake, a single tree flickering.

Part I

1

"I have to meet James," I say to Doug. Doug does not say anything. I'm glad Doug does not say anything. Doug is a dog, and it would have been terrifying if he did.

I put on my coat, and my phone alerts me to a text message. It's from Abby:

If you're going to meet James, please try to get me another assignment.

I tell her OK. I pet Doug on the head and open the blinds so Doug can look out the window. I turn on the fan for white noise so Doug does not go berserk from odd sounds, whistles or chirpings. I walk out the door to my apartment and down the old wooden twisting staircase and out the front door. I live in one of those old colonial homes that has been chopped into apartments.

The trees are orange and red, and the air is clean with autumn, which I find cleaner than spring. Towns in Connecticut are alive with fall. This season is one of the few times during the year people are friendly to each other. Another time is when the town celebrates itself and the people are filled with town pride for no other reason than they have town pride.

There are banners hanging on stores and streetlamps and spanning across streets. Every weekend, there are festivals, and I'm reminded that even in what some consider to be small towns there is a wealth of resources surrounding us in all the cities. There are parking bans so equipment can pass in spite of the narrow streets. Much of the festivals' equipment comes from New Haven, Hartford and Bridgeport, though some comes from New York City and Boston. As much as city people want the world to become like the city, they also want the town to remain the town and invest money to keep it that way. Some of us are grateful. Most of us are suspicious.

#

I walk into the café where I'm meeting James, order a cup of coffee and sit down at a table. I'm fifteen minutes early. James will not be here for another twenty.

I put my phone on silent and see more texts from Abby. One says:

By another assignment I mean a different assignment.

The next says:

Something other than city council meetings and ribbon cuttings.

The third says:

Let me know you read these before you meet with James, otherwise I'm coming down there.

I tell her OK and not to worry. I put the phone on silent and put it into my pocket.

James arrives. He has the sort of desperate look on his face you might expect of a sloth escaping a blazing forest. He is not often full of energy except when talking about new assignments, and I can see this is on his mind. He orders coffee and walks to me and before he is seated he is already off, "I can't stay long but hear me out. This is the most exclusive show in America—no, the world—no, the *history of theater*, and I'm asking you to cover it," he says.

"No," I reply, already aware of where the conversation is heading, "I'm not reviewing a local play. I don't know anything about theater or drama." I pretend to think for a moment. "Why don't you get Abby to do it? You know how much she loves city council meetings and ribbon cuttings." James is a theater junkie. He once asked me to cover an elementary school recital by homeschoolers.

"This isn't a review," he counters. "This is a kind of interest piece, and I need details. Abby doesn't give the kind of details you give."

"You said that was a good thing."

He drinks his coffee and pauses, thinking. "When did I say that?"

"Last week," I say, "You told me I give too many details and that I should try to write more like Abby."

"Look." He leans forward, elbows on the table. "Abby's work isn't where it needs to be, and she doesn't seem to be improving."

I know he is right. I'm already aware that I will have to explain this conversation to Abby gently. My silence is my response.

"Let me first tell you what this is before you say no," he says.

"OK."

"Once every sixty years a theater in upstate New York puts together an elaborate worldwide production. Set designers, actors, producers, stage managers, makeup artists, choreographers and directors from London, New York, Milan and Melbourne are brought in. They even bring in their own front of house workers and clean-up crew. It's like those low-key dinner parties organized by serious foodies and chefs, except it's for serious theater-goers. It's called *Goat-Song*."

"Never heard of it."

"It's not the name of the play; it's the name of the event."

"Still."

"The play changes with every production."

"What are they doing this time?" I ask.

"I don't know. No one knows until the night of the performance."

I lean back and cross my arms. "Upstate New York?"

"Yeah. Brookings." James gives me a half-knowing look with an intentionally half-covered poker face. He is waiting for me to broach the subject. He will not admit what we are thinking if I do not admit it first. Conversation for him is a game that he intends to win.

I'm about to bring up the issue with New York and decide against it. "If you're so interested, why aren't you doing it?" I ask.

He seems disappointed that I'm not playing but he recovers quickly. "That's the same week of the spelling bee nationals. I already have a plane ticket, credentials and hotel reservations under my name. Besides, I don't want someone to go and watch a play and leave. I want you there gathering as much information as you can. This'll be a multi-week serial, maybe even a book. That's why I need details."

I drink more coffee and look around the room, mulling all of this over.

James gives me one last pitch. "The production is put on by something like a hundred of the greatest theater artists of our time. There are only two-thousand seats available worldwide, and you can't buy them."

"Then how did you get one?"

"I entered a lottery to send a reviewer and won."

"You said it wasn't a review."

James looks at his watch. "Just think about it. I have to go." He stands up, drinks the rest of his coffee and puts on his coat. "We need your details," he says, wagging a finger at me, and he walks out the door.

James is the editor of a small weekly with a staff made up of James, Abby and myself. James edits and writes a few stories and columns, Abby and I fill the rest of the paper reporting on local events. Every Monday, James and I wake up early and deliver the paper. I would say James treats the paper like his baby, but that might give the impression he abuses children. It's better not to compare the way he treats the paper to a relationship with something living.

Every week, we meet for coffee in Café Allen to discuss work. Café Allen is a hipster shop, one of those places where the coffee tastes so local you cannot tell if it is good or bad, and the last place you would expect someone like James, who once referred to the fads of young people as "puberty discharges." Abby met with us until she had an episode, and we could not contact her for a week. Her reporting was amateurish to begin with, but after that she became worse. James seems uncertain if she will continue with the paper, but he keeps her on for now.

The café suddenly lights with chattering and murmurs. A young couple whisper to each other, pointing out the large windows at the front of the shop. Some teenagers take out their cell phones and record what they see.

James runs back into the café, grabs me by the arm, lifts me out of my seat and hurries me toward the window.

"That's part of the set for *Goat-Song*. These are the designers from Boston on their way to New York," he says.

"Why are they driving through town and not on the highways?"

James does not respond, and I suspect he may have had something to do with it.

There are three semi trucks driving by. Each is carrying sets and props for the show. James was right to call the production elaborate.

The first truck carries only one piece. It is of the sky, vivid with Floridian pastels, but there are three suns: one green, one blue and one purple. The suns are in different positions in the sky and their reflections splay over hyper-real water. As the truck slowly drives, the water comes alive, moving, shimmering and reflecting the suns in an unexplainable illusion. The second truck carries a couple pieces. One is an enormous marionette, both an artist's masterpiece and a child's nightmare. The truck also carries what appear to be live mature oak trees as well as a rustic wooden shed. The third truck carries livestock, living and breathing livestock, not merely ornamentation: sheep and horses and cattle. There are no goats.

James claps his hands in excitement. He pats me on the shoulder, mutters something unintelligible and exits the café. The murmurs die down now that the excitement is out of sight.

A young woman busses the table. One of her earlobes is two-pronged, a broken loop, the result of over-enlarging with gauges. I think she catches me staring but I'm not sure. I feel bad but give neither wisdom nor condolence. It is the kind of accident that will make you think twice before discharging puberty.

#

I exit the café and check my phone. There is another text from Abby:

Well?

The time-stamp reveals this message was sent ten minutes after my meeting with James started, though Abby knows that I put my phone on silent when I meet with James.

Working on it. Some kind of play review.

Abby responds immediately:

Play review?

Yes, I tell her, and I put my phone in my pocket. I head home to do some work. I leave the phone on silent.

I arrive at my place, open the entry door, walk up the old wooden steps and unlock the door to my apartment. There is an odor and I wonder if one of my neighbors is cleaning or is letting their trash sit by their front door. When I open my door, it becomes obvious that the smell is coming from inside my apartment.

It is hard to tell if what I'm seeing is really what I'm seeing. This is what I see: Doug is dead, and even though Doug has been alone for about two hours, it looks as if he has been dead for days. He is decomposing. Half of his body is deformed as if he were hit by something.

There is a tunnel-vision shock that comes upon me. I try to think of what to do next and unreasonably the words of Blaise Pascal are all that come to mind:

All of humanity's problems stem from man's inability to sit quietly in a room alone.

2

There is a legend about Dmitri Shostakovich, the 20th century Russian composer. One day Joseph Stalin called for Shostakovich. When Shostakovich entered Stalin's chambers, Stalin ordered everyone but Shostakovich out of the room. Stalin motioned for Shostakovich to sit, which he did, and then Stalin stood and picked up a silver tray, on which stood two glasses filled with vodka.

Shostakovich was suspicious about the drink. Stalin did not quell Shostakovich's suspicion when Stalin did not give Shostakovich a choice but chose his drink for him. Shostakovich managed a smile, closed his eyes and drank it all.

Stalin smiled. Stalin drank, licked the inside of the glass, peered into it to make sure it was finished and set the drink down. Stalin pulled out his chair and sat down. "Comrade," he said, "your music inspires me."

"Thank you," said Shostakovich.

"I find your music to be all that can keep unwanted images out of my head. It is a great relief. I often listen to your music after many days of difficulty so I can move onto future difficulty."

Shostakovich was surprised to hear this. He did not know how to respond. The beauty of his music wiped clean past atrocities in order for future ones to be committed. He bowed his head and said nothing.

"That is all," said Stalin.

Shostakovich stood, pushed in his chair, bowed once more to Stalin. He opened the door, but before he stepped out, Stalin said something. Shostakovich slowly turned his head and looked at Stalin, who motioned for Shostakovich to return. Shostakovich closed the door and walked back.

Stalin smiled. "Did you think I was going to kill you?" he asked.

"In all honesty, yes," replied Shostakovich.

"Don't worry about that," said Stalin. "If I wanted you dead, I wouldn't poison you. I would shoot you in your head in your sleep."

After a small pause, Stalin added, "And it would have already happened."

#

I'm lying on my back on the floor of my apartment, hands behind my head. Shostakovich's *Second Waltz* is playing. Today is my day off, which means I will be asked to work.

The song is haunting. It is a work of beauty in a time of death and power. Change and transition are the heart of the piece. Shostakovich is reaching out of a culture of paranoia and blood and clawing the royal coat of the tsar. And yet it is a rejection of the lavishness of the tsar, resembling a dictator's military marching piece. One could just as easily use this song to march the streets in praise of Stalin as they could use it to dance in riches and ornamentation in the presence of the tsar. Maybe most profound of all is what the song marks in modern history: the death of royalty. The trench between the kingdom and the state is wide and filled with corpses. This song is one of many corpses between the royal palace and the department of labor.

There is the sound of a large truck unleashing its horn. Out the window there is a semi truck carrying more set pieces. They are set pieces for a dungeon: wood and iron cages and medieval torture devices. People crowd the truck, preventing it from passing safely. The people are not hostile. They have phones in their hands and are shamelessly angling for the best photos and videos. The truck driver rolls down his window with dwindling patience and begs them to move. They pay no attention. The crowd walks back to the sidewalk and the truck passes. They look at their phones, examining their prizes.

There is another sound at the window in the kitchen. The sound is faint and unexpected, and I cannot identify it immediately. I walk into the kitchen and there is a black cat on the outside of the window patting the glass, asking to come inside. I'm about to tap the pane to scare the cat away when I realize three things. The first is that we are on the second floor. I do not know how the cat climbed to this spot. The second is that, if I spook the cat, it may fall onto cement from here. The third is that this looks like Abby's cat. It has the same white patch of fur on its head and the same-colored collar.

I open the window and let the cat in. I prevent it from coming too far inside and examine its tags. The tag reads: *Horatio. Return to Abby Edwards, 95 Rose Way.* Abby lives nearly two miles from here and neither the cat nor Abby have been to my apartment before, though I have been to hers. I put the cat in a box, shut the lid in a four-sided tape-less pattern, walk to my car and drive to Abby's.

#

Abby lives in a townhouse with a roommate named Colleen. I have not met Colleen, but Abby told me much about her. I got the impression that they are roommates and nothing more. Aristotle would call their friendship one of utility.

I arrive at Abby's and, looking at her house, I wonder if there will ever come a time in my life when I imagine something correctly before I see it. The cat is calm and has not squirmed much during the ride over. I carry the box and walk to the front door and ring the doorbell. Two doors down there is an elderly woman gardening a small flowerbed in front of her door. She does not turn her head to look but is carefully paying attention.

A young woman answers the door. Her face is red, and she is wiping away tears and mucus with tissue. She says nothing but waits for me to speak first as if she has already asked who I am and what I want.

"Are you Colleen?" I ask.

She nods.

"Is Abby here?" I ask.

She shakes her head. The redness in her face livens. More tears come.

"I have her cat," I say, holding up the box.

Colleen shakes her head more, which I do not understand, and she wipes more tears and mucus from her face and finally speaks. "Abby isn't here," she says.

"Do you know when—"

As soon as I begin the question, she shakes her head and says, "She won't be back." Colleen wipes tears from her eyes one last time and throws the tissue into a small garbage can. She takes a turbulent and guttural breath and speaks, "Abby was in an accident last night."

The cat squirms in the box. The lid is closed but the cat is trying to peer through the center slit. I put one hand over the lid to keep the cat from escaping.

"Which hospital is she in?" I ask.

"She's dead," Colleen says, squashing further misunderstandings. It is painful for her to be this blunt. She grabs another tissue.

"I have her cat—" I say, and before I say more, Colleen shakes her head and shuts the door. There is a brief pause, and the deadbolt turns. Colleen walks from the door. There is only silence from inside.

I set the box on the ground to rest my arms. The elderly gardener is looking at me. "Do you want a cat?" I ask her. She smiles and resumes gardening. Her smile is neither a gentle nor a sympathetic smile. It is a smile masking her condescension. She sees me as yet another young person weaseling out of responsibility. And maybe she is right.

2.5

Abby Edwards's spirit fell and unfolded. She was caught in timeless being. She felt neither pain nor happiness nor fear. But she was aware. Her spirit unraveled in spiraled ribbons as she fell through layers of light.

Her memory was slow to surface. She did not remember the moments leading to her death, but she knew that she was dead. For a moment, it was all she knew, until the memories

of her previous life rose in her. Existence after death was familiar yet foreign. In many ways it was as she imagined it,
and yet it was different than anything she could have imagined.

Abby continued her descent and saw the surface beneath
her. It was an enormous plane, parts resembling hard but
flowing water, other parts resembling valleys and mountains. It was not a planet but a flat plane, and from this height
she saw the edges of the plane, under which lurked a great
abyss. She wondered what would happen when she hit the
plane.

Her spirit stopped unfolding and started to mend. The
layers of light healed her and infused her with life. As she
came together, her descent slowed, and she found herself
standing on the plane with neither harm nor surprise.

There were geometrical shapes of different kinds and
sizes traveling the plane, like precious stones, clear as glass,
in deep hues of greens and blues. Music shimmered and
hummed from them, rich as chimes and complex as sym-
phonies.

"This is beauty," she thought to herself. The knowledge
of beauty was one which eluded her. A faint memory from
her childhood came to mind. She was in an art museum, staring at a work, searching for the location of the work's beauty.

To her surprise, a myriad of the geometrical shapes took
notice of her. They rushed and built a giant wall in front of
her, the top reaching beyond her sight. The shapes fit togeth-

er, their sides in perfect alignment with no gaps. One shape, a triangle, jangled and rang, making a tone. Then a second followed. Then a third. Soon the wall came alive in waves of sound and light as it played the tune of a waltz. It was Shostakovich's *Second Waltz*.

She knew the song from when she was little. She was nine. Her father took her to a father-daughter dance. The school gymnasium was anything but elegant, yet her father bought her a dress and rented a tuxedo and they danced in the joy of their relationship. After the death of her father, that song became the chest that hid the memory of her father. It was a chest she rarely opened. Now, though, there was no pain or despair when she thought of him but only love.

The waltz ended. Near the base of the wall, a crack formed in the center, and a fluid doorway opened. The opening revealed a figure standing on the other side.

Abby approached the figure, which remained motionless, though it was clearly alive. The figure was a shade of black, a shadow, in stark contrast to the colors and lights that filled this world. She moved cautiously toward it, for the first time feeling a sense of fear or uneasiness.

She came within reaching distance of the shadow. There was a glass wall between her and the shadow. She saw that the figure was as a three-dimensional opaque shadow with a human likeness. She put her hand to the glass and felt its cool crystal hardness. She put her hand down. The figure took a step toward her and walked through the glass as if it were water, startling Abby. Abby tripped as she backed away from the shadow. Her spirit became undone. The shadow grabbed her spirit of ribbons, and her spirit came together, wrapping around the shadow figure. The two became one.

When the process finished, she looked at her hands. She had a sturdiness and a power she did not have as a mere spirit. The wall of shapes lost their light and life. They faded from greens and blues to plain glass, and they collapsed, shattering on the ground.

The surface of the plane shook with rumbling and roaring. A host—her host—of creatures approached from across the plane. They were small and large, winged and striped, some mammalian, some reptilian, creatures of all sorts and colors, mesmerizing, beautiful. They gathered before her and their presence stretched beyond what Abby could see, an ocean of life, of animals. Thousands of them, on the ground and in the air, gathered before her.

"I am a god," she realized. "And these are my subjects." The sea of creatures bowed.

<u>3</u>

"You're kidding."

"No," I say to James. "I just spoke to Abby's roommate. She was in an accident last night and was killed."

"D—s...fa—...w?"

"You're cutting out," I say. "Hold on, I'm driving home, I'm almost there."

James pauses and waits. I pull into my parking spot and keep the car running.

"OK, what did you say?"

"I asked if her family knows," he says.

"I didn't ask. I assume so, if her roommate knows."

James sighs. His sigh is a cocktail of emotions: sudden loss, sympathy, frustration from inconvenience. He does not vocalize this last emotion, but it is clearly present. He is an employer with unexpected immediate extra work.

"Jamie," he says, and the use of my first name catches my attention. James has lived in Connecticut all his adult life, but he is from the West Coast, which shows in his rare use of first names. He is no longer requesting or even pleading. He is begging.

"Have you given more thought to *Goat-Song*? I know it's Upstate," he sighs again, "but I don't have anyone else." This is partly an apology for our earlier conversation which he made into a game. I have rarely heard James beg. I have never heard him apologize.

Horatio is in the box with the lid open. He is looking at me. "O—" I begin, and I stop because as I speak the cat leans forward in suspense as if he understands what is happening and it disturbs me. But I finish. "OK."

"Thank you," says James. I know it is the first and the last time I will hear him say those words. "I'll email you the pro-

duction info I have. I'll also email you the little bit of back-
ground I have to kickstart your research—which I highly rec-
ommend doing."

"Thanks," I say.

James hangs up. I turn off the car and I look at Horatio.
"I can't tell if you're pleased or displeased," I say to him. And
then I say, "Not sure I'd like to meet the person who can."

#

I walk into my place and let Horatio out of the box. The
stench of Doug is nearly gone though there is a faint trace of
decomposing flesh. I designate two bowls for Horatio. One I
fill with water, the other with canned chicken from my
Nor'easter emergency supply. I leave them on the floor and
start researching my new assignment.

I open my email and check the information James sent
me. *Goat-Song*, it turns out, has roots in Greek theater. In its
name, at least. In Greek, the word for *tragedy* is a compound
word made up of the words *goat* and *song*. There is a lot of
speculation about how this came to be the word for tragedy,
many sources referencing goat skins and goat sacrifices. This
does not surprise me. The word *Goat-Song* leaves a pagan
flavor on the tongue when spoken.

This is the extent of James's investigation, and I fare no
better. There is little to be found on the history of the production. I cannot find the businesses that supply their mate-

rial for sets and props. I cannot find past reviews in papers. I cannot find the lottery James entered, though this is barely worth noting. James said that this is a clandestine affair, and he finds his way into these things regularly. He once entered a contest for a lock of hair which was advertised as "from an actress unnamed" with the lock "to be retrieved tonight."

I am pushed to my last resort: extremist online forums. There I find whispers about *Goat-Song*. A few pictures of trucks carrying set pieces. One is a modern photo of a polaroid of a set piece taken from the previous production sixty years ago. The piece in the polaroid is of an enormous multicolored Chinese-style dragon. Another user uploaded a video of the three-suns set piece I saw drive by the café. No surprise, the forum is full of conspiracy theories about *Goat-Song*, ranging from presidential mind control to the creation of Jewish holidays.

A throaty sound breaks into my awareness, and I realize the cat is about to vomit. I run to the cat and lift him from the carpet and carry him to the hardwood as his dry heaves hold increasing promise. I close my eyes, not wanting to see the vomit as it comes out. But instead of a wet splatter, there is the sound of tinkling chimes. I open my eyes and see a small geometric glass shaped like a many-sided die, glowing a faint green. It hums and chimes rich melodies.

<u>4</u>

Today is Abby's funeral. James and I were invited. James declined; he has too much work at the moment without Abby. I accepted. Seems odd to claim her cat but not attend her funeral. Seems odder still to have ethical standards toward the dead. This last thought I keep to myself.

The funeral is in Massachusetts, just outside Springfield. The scenery is beautiful, and the drive is unpleasant. You may not know this: the road to hell is not only paved with good intentions, but it is also any number of highways traversing the lower three New England states.

I finish packing and give my suitcase a once over to see if I have forgotten anything. What is packed will last me for the next few days. After the funeral, I will head to New York to begin covering *Goat-Song*. James and I agreed that I should arrive early to begin research, especially if he wants to turn this into a book.

I load everything into my car and walk to my downstairs neighbor's door and knock. The apartment is occupied by Donna, a single mother, and her teenage daughter Stephanie. Donna answers the door.

"You all set?" she asks.

"Yes. Here's the key and instructions and some money for Stephanie. Tell her thanks."

"I will," she says.

"The cat's a cat, so she doesn't need to do much. Empty the litter box, food and water. If you have any questions, give me a call."

Horatio watches me from the window as I get into my car. Donna waves at me and steps inside her apartment. I make a quick stop to fill up with gas and then drive to Massachusetts.

#

I pull into Harley's Funeral Home and park the car. There are a decent number of attendees. They walk across the parking lot and into the funeral home in clusters. There is a valet who is overwhelmed and has given up. He is behind the building smoking a cigarette, peeking around the corner every so often. The weather is turning colder so the funeral is indoors. I pull the geometric glass figure from my pocket. It no longer sings or glows. It has not made a sound since Horatio first coughed it up.

The funeral is a wake with a Catholic flavor. We have been told in advance there will be no ceremony or eulogy. This is merely a gathering for friends and family to remember Abby. There is, however, a kneeler in front of the casket and it is used in observance by almost every mourner who enters before they talk to one another.

The only person in the room I recognize is Colleen, Abby's roommate. She sees me and waves, and I nod back. I give my condolences to Abby's mom. She does not know who I am, and I do not introduce myself.

Before I leave, I approach the casket. I look in and see that it is Abby. Odd that I need to affirm her death to myself. There is a part of me that hoped that I would look in and, to the amazement of all, declare that there has been some mistake, that this is the wrong body. But there is no mistake. There is no mix-up. This is her, and she is dead and that is that.

The finality of death strikes me harder when it is someone younger than me, and I do not know why. I suppose it is because when it is someone older than me, I think *it will happen,* but when it is someone younger than me I think *it could have already happened.* Funny how future inevitability is less striking than past possibility.

I give a smile to Abby's corpse that conveys something like *I'm sorry this happened to you, and I wish it didn't.* I put my hand on the casket as a substitute for putting my hand on her hand, which I cannot bring myself to do. Then I hear a soft chiming.

I look around, and no one else seems to hear it. The glass die in my pocket is chiming. Its color returned, and it is pulsing and humming.

The director, hearing the chiming, walks to me. "Sir, please take your phone call in the hall or outside."

"OK," I say. He smiles at me firmly and walks alongside me, escorting me out of the room. I walk not only out of the room but out of the building and to my car. I take off my tie and my coat, get into my car and begin to make my way to New York.

4.5

Abby Edwards sat on her throne in her palace and surveyed her work. She modeled it after the Palace of Versailles, which she studied extensively in college during the two semesters she considered a career in architecture. When she first arrived in this new world, memories of her past were slow to boil to the top, but now she had near perfect recall of every detail. Effortlessly, she imagined in minutest detail Versailles, and although she recreated aspects of it, this palace was wholly her own.

There were banquet halls for feasts of celebration, amphitheaters for serenity and art, pools for joy and laughter. She was particularly proud of the ballroom she designed. She could not tell if she spent one hour or ten thousand years building it. It was based on the ballroom she imagined when she was a child dancing with her father in the school gymnasium. It no longer existed only in the imagination of a child but in her newly founded queendom. It was a monument to pure imagination and the creative act.

The creatures of her world deeply loved her. They gladly submitted to her rule and reign. For them, she was a righteous and a just queen who guarded and protected them. She was not, as is often the case with rulers, the guardian of their bodies, to keep pain at bay. She was more. She was the guardian of their being. Their lives, essences, experiences and awareness were all under her guardianship.

"It is time," she said, sitting on her throne. "My palace is finished. And I will have a new name. From now and forever I will be Queen Amarantha, for all that unfolds from now to eternity will be unfading, and it will be beauty and hope." The creatures in her palace bowed and worshiped.

But there was one creature who did not bow. This did not escape Queen Amarantha's attention. She stood from her throne and approached the creature. The other creatures cleared a path for her. The one creature, undaunted, looked at her. "My queen," it said, "there is an army approaching."

"Show me," she said.

The creature gave a slight bow and led her to the entrance gate of her palace. The creature bowed deeply as it opened the heavy door. Queen Amarantha stepped forward in wonder as she saw a great storm cloud in the distance. The cloud moved toward the palace with glows of reds and purples. Lightning struck the plane from the cloud so frequently it looked as if they were the legs on which the cloud walked.

"Find shelter and safety for the little ones," she said, "and instruct the others to prepare for battle."

An angelic creature flew over her head and encompassed her palace blasting its horn.

Part II

1

The traffic is bad until Albany and Schenectady. After Schenectady I begin to relax. I opt for the less direct state route instead of the interstate for the rest of the drive. It is colder here, but the roads are not yet dangerous. Unless you count a deer hoofing you in the face through the windshield dangerous.

Now that I'm through the traffic, I think about Abby, and the deeper I go into the trees and the lakes my thoughts of Abby turn to Sarah.

I come to the spot where the marker once was. At first, I consider passing by, but the mere fact that I'm here gets the better of me, and I pull over. The marker is faded but still standing. It reads:

In memory of our darling Sarah.

Beyond the marker is the lake and in the lake are the bones of my daughter.

A vehicle pulls up next to me. "Jamie?"

It is a large truck. A man sits in the driver's seat. Faith steps out of the truck. "What are you doing here?" she asks. She rubs her arms from the cold.

"I'm passing through on an assignment," I say.

Faith looks at me, still in disbelief.

"It was an emergency," I explain, "one of our reporters died and I had to cover."

There is a pity in her eyes that I cannot escape. It is not a pity of the triumphant condescending to the weak. It is the pity shared by those who have been mutually ground down and humiliated by life. My pity is her pity. We have both suffered the same. She is looking at me in the same way she looks at herself in the mirror.

"It wasn't Abby, was it?" Faith asks.

I'm surprised that Faith is aware of writers for the paper. For a moment, I consider asking her how she knows of Abby, but I refrain. Instead, I nod. Faith immediately understands and has already pieced the situation together. She needs no further clarification.

Faith points across the road at a tavern and says, "Why don't you come to the bar with us?" It is a small wooden building. It has curtains but they are drawn, and I cannot see inside.

"That's all right," I say, and I try to smile.

"It was good to see you," she says. She is about to say more but hesitates. She climbs into the truck. Faith speaks to the man. He tries not to look at me as they drive across the street and park at the bar.

I decide to do something emotionally foolish at this point. I get inside my car and put on Shostakovich's *Second Waltz*. I am immediately deluged with the memory of dancing with Sarah in the gymnasium at her school for a father-daughter dance.

I feel her standing on my feet as we waltz. I see her joy and pride as she wears her new dress. She closes her eyes, and she is in love with me and with this moment. She has no interest in her classmates. She is not concerned with whether they are watching her or whether she will be made fun of the next day. She only has eyes for me. I only have eyes for her. And we are dancing.

The song ends. I'm back in my car looking at the lake. I need to regain myself before continuing to drive, so I leave my car and cross the street and enter the bar for a drink.

#

The tavern reeks of cigarettes. Smoking indoors has been illegal for almost twenty years and I would bet money no one has smoked in here at least for the last ten. Not because they care about the law but because there is a new generation, a non-smoking generation, coming up in society, one that cannot see deeper than material ethics, raging against the pollution of the body while relishing the pollution of the intellect.

The bartender is a woman in her fifties. She greets me with that peculiar northeast indifference rooted in honest contempt. Up here, customer-service friendliness is viewed as dishonest, because no one is happy-go-lucky when life is this bad. It is also a sign of weakness here, a defense mechanism of the cowardly, of those too scared to fight or to flee.

"An IPA," I say, "whatever you have is fine."

"Any food?" she asks. I shake my head no. She pours the beer and gives it to me. "Open tab?" she asks. I shake my head no and give her some cash.

Faith and her guy are sitting at a table in the back. The guy sees me. He and I make eye contact, and he sits up and leans forward and says something to her. He drinks the rest of his beer—three-fourths of a glass—stands up, puts on his hat and walks out. He looks me in the eyes intentionally for the first time, and he nods at me as he leaves, and I cannot tell if he is being friendly or unsociable.

The beer is good and almost immediately I feel myself coming back after thinking too much about Sarah. Faith sits beside me. She orders another beer and hands her empty glass to the bartender.

"So, what're you writing about this time?" she asks.

"Wombats," I say. "Been an infestation."

The bartender gets a fearful look in her eyes as she tries not to let on that she is listening.

"Don't kid," says Faith.

"I'm not. Australian exchange students brought them in. Put them in dresses and called them 'fair dinkum science specimens.'"

"How'd they get through customs?"

"Anyone who speaks about science and has an accent gets a free pass in this country."

Faith looks into her glass and smiles. "Fine," she says. "Don't tell me."

She drinks more of her fresh glass of beer. It becomes obvious Faith feels obligated to be around me, and maybe she even wants to be around me, but she has run out of things to say because we have an unwritten code not to speak about the unspeakable things between us. We sit next to each other in silence as we drink together. After a few minutes she finishes and gives the glass and some cash to the bartender.

"I better get going," she says, "Norm is waiting for me in the truck. He wanted to give us a couple minutes alone."

She stands and opens the door.

"Faith," I say, and she turns and looks at me. "Thank you." I don't know what I'm thankful for, but my thankfulness is not insincere. She smiles and she walks out the door.

The bartender leans over the counter to me. She has an anxious look on her face. "Wombats?"

"Yeah," I say. "Big ones," and I counterfeit their size with my hands.

#

I intentionally wait until Faith and Norm leave before I walk out. I finish the last of my beer and watch them drive away. A motorhome parks in front of the tavern.

The motorhome is enormous and sleek, donning California plates. A large man steps out—large both ways—and he looks around at the trees and the lake with the excitement of a child. A tiny woman—tiny both ways—descends the stairs behind him. He is overly dressed, unaccustomed to cool autumns, wearing a thick cotton plaid shirt and a heavy jacket. She is bundled in a wool scarf and a heavy coat and a hat. They walk inside the tavern.

"Man," the man says, "what a great drive. Really nice." He looks at the bartender, "The trees you have around here do not disappoint. We haven't been this way since we went to Niagara on our honeymoon. That was, what, thirty-three years ago?" His wife nods. She's a mousy thing, getting mousier by the second as she unravels her bundle. "We're on our way to Brookings, and we're a little lost. No cell service, and the missus here accidentally shut off the GPS app trying to change the music."

At the name of Brookings, my ears perk. There is nothing special about Brookings like there is about, say, Cooperstown. It seems likely they will be attending *Goat-Song*.

"I have a map," I say. I hope to get some information from them about the play. Or at least an interesting interview if they are attending.

The man smiles wildly. "That'd be great."

"One second." I exit the bar, cross the road, grab the map from my car and return. I open it and show them where we are and the route that heads to Brookings.

"Listen," he says, "I want to thank you. Come into the camper and let me thank you properly." The wife smiles and nods as she begins re-bundling, wrapping her thick scarf around her face even though she just finished unbundling.

"OK," I say. We step out of the tavern. He opens his motorhome and I step inside.

It is a modern home on wheels, fancier than my apartment. There are stainless steel appliances, a flatscreen TV and an island in the central kitchen area. In the back there are stairs that lead to a bedroom.

"Sit down, sit down," he says as he clears a place for me at the table. "What's your name?"

"Jamie."

"Mine's Tom, and this is my wife, Maddie." Tom steps aside for a moment. I nod hello at Maddie, who is unraveling her bundle again. She finishes and hangs the scarf on a wooden peg next to the door. For the first time, I get a real look at her and her face is so small that I cannot remember it when I look away.

Tom sets crystals and rocks on the table in front of me. Then a small round glass ball. He sits, and he is wearing a small turban. I did not expect this. These are the kind of details James loves. It will likely make for a good read.

It goes like this: Tom closes his eyes, while Maddie, on cue, slides black canvas against the inside of the windshield, draws the curtains and hangs black drapes over the windows, blocking out most of the outside light. She does this with an ease and fluidity that speaks to repetition. A flame broaches the darkness. Tom lights two candles on the table. Maddie begins to hum deeply. In mere moments, I'm thrust into a ceremony.

"I've never had my fortune read," I say.

"No," says Tom. His joviality is gone, and he is deeply somber. All is heavy around me. "This isn't a reading. This is a séance."

Maddie is humming and it dawns on me that she is humming Shostakovich's *Second Waltz*. The rocks, crystal and glass glow and chime in accordance with the song. A chiming sound comes from my pocket. The geometric glass die is glowing green and chiming in time with the crystal and rocks.

Tom hums along with Maddie. And I hear the music as if a symphony were playing softly in the parking lot. I become so convinced that there is a symphony outside that I pull back the curtain on the window to see it.

I look in awe as I see water. It is as if the motorhome is submerged, like we are in a submarine deep in a well-lit ocean. Schools of fish swim by. Turtles glide. The water is rich and bright blue, alive with marine life whose movements are beautifully aligned with the music. Just as I begin to wonder if this is a video screen instead of a window, I notice that water is seeping through the window, dripping onto the bench seat and the table. I am not convinced that this is not some kind of elaborate illusion, and I search for the water's source.

Then the music stops. Tom and Maddie stop humming. There is a disturbing silence. And then there is a muffled splash above us. In the window I see legs, human legs, kicking, the current pulling the person downward. And it is my Sarah. She reaches upward and a hand grabs her hand, but she is dragged downward. She is trying to swim to the surface, but she cannot. She stops fighting. She sees me, and she moves to the window and she looks at me in the motorhome. She beats her hands on the window, trying to get through. The window cracks. She sees the crack, and she beats it again. The window cracks more. Once more and her fist breaks through the window. Water pours in violently. She grabs my hand, and I try to hold her, but her skin is wet and slick and I cannot find a grip. She sinks below the window.

The water level lowers, and we are in the tavern parking lot.

There are water weeds and a couple of fish on the floor of the motorhome. There is an inch or two of standing water. The fish flop and gasp for air.

"I need to lie down," says Tom, and he ascends the steps, dizzy, bumping into the wall, and he walks to his bedroom and shuts the door.

"What was that?" I say, and as I walk toward him, Maddie puts her hand on my chest to stop me and she shakes her head. "What was that?" I repeat, angry and confused. Maddie opens the door. Water drains out of the door and onto the parking lot. In my hand is the geometric die. It is no longer glowing or humming, but it is dead again. I put it in my pocket, walk out of the motorhome and cross the street to my car. I grab a change of clothes from my suitcase in the trunk, staring at the motorhome, waiting for something to happen. But nothing happens. I step into the back of my car and change in the cramped space, putting the wet clothes on the floor. I exit and walk around and enter the driver's seat.

I stepped into the tavern to calm myself and now I am more undone than before. I start my car and resume the drive to Brookings. The motorhome, also heading to Brookings, pulls out of the parking lot and follows me. I quickly outpace them and lose sight of them. There is an irrational determination and urge to fight that possesses me to protect me from fully understanding that, once again, life has humiliated me.

My hand touched her hand. I almost had her this time.

2

The further you travel Upstate, the more the evergreen trees encroach on the deciduous trees, both in quantity and in height. The atmosphere here is a braid of lore and history, and as you drive up the state the mood changes from the fairy tales of the Woods of Western Europe to the half-believable folklore of the Forests of Canada. The line between history and lore becomes increasingly erased, transitioning from the clearer distinction of pixies and elves to the messier blur of sasquatches and lake monsters. There is no distinction between mythology and history. There is history and there are rumors, and the rumors are true.

It is dark outside. My high beams are on, but I must be cautious as they reflect the autumn mist settling from the Adirondacks. I spent too many daylight hours at Abby's funeral, the tavern and the motorhome, and now the last leg of the trip must be made in the dark. I have not seen another vehicle for the last thirty minutes, and I'm anxious to be in my hotel.

Somewhere near Lake Placid my engine light comes on. It catches my eye in the dark. I hit something in the split second I take my eyes off the road to look at the light. I quickly look up and see only my hood, which is bent in the front with its center blocking my view. I slow down, aware enough not to slam my brakes and go into a skid, guessing as best as I can when I am on the shoulder of the road.

The car is stopped. I put it in park and set the emergency brake. I grab a small flashlight from the glove compartment and step out of the car.

I first examine the car's position. It is not fully on the shoulder of the road. Half of the car is over the shoulder's line and half of the car is in the driving lane. This is a good thing. The shoulder is barely wide enough for a car and there is a steep slope careening into the forest. There is an old wood-and-wire fence to protect cars from going down the slope. There is a hole in the fence that has not been repaired from when a car apparently broke through. My car is perfectly aligned to drive through the hole in the fence.

I stand by the driver's side door and shine the small flashlight at the side and hood of the car. There is steam or smoke pouring from under the hood. It is cold enough that I cannot tell which it is. The hood is shaped like a pitched tent. A sudden vibration rattles the hood, and the source of the vibration comes from the front of the car.

I slowly step around the car toward the front. The flashlight first reveals a leg. It is moving. It looks like it is covered in fur. The light from the flashlight catches on the ground, and, startled, I shine it to the ground to see what it is that caught the light. It is blood. I shine the light back to the front of the car. As I approach the front of the car, I hear a whining sound. I finish circling to the front of the car and see that there is a dog stuck in the front bumper.

The dog's collar is on the ground. I pick it up and it reads: *Doug*. It is my dead dog. There is a horror that overcomes me. A tremor goes through his body, and then he is lifeless.

I'm not thinking clearly. I rush inside my car and try to start it, intending fully to drive into town with a dog stuck in the bumper. The engine will not turn. Tears form in my eyes as the day's events and hopelessness sets in.

Something taps on the passenger window. I'm relieved, thinking it is a passerby. The passenger door opens. It is not a passerby. It is something else altogether. It is a black humanoid, otherworldly, like a mannequin dipped in ink. It has no face and yet it is looking at me, bent at its waist with its head and torso leaning into the cab of the car, one hand anchored on the roof.

It is looking at me.

I cannot scream. I cannot move. I cannot understand.

And still it is looking at me.

Headlights pierce my rear windshield and shine on the humanoid, who disappears as if the light revealed the illusion for what it is. A car stops next to me. A man quickly gets out.

"Are you OK?" he asks.

I shake my head no.

The man walks closer. "Are you hurt?"

I shake my head no.

"OK then," he says. "Can you get out of the car?"

I'm shaking, but I step out. He helps me up. The blood on the pavement is gone. I walk toward the front of the car. For one moment, he almost tries to stop me, but he lets me. Doug is gone. There is an indentation in my hood but nothing more.

The man walks to me. "What did you hit?" he asks.

"I don't know," I say. My throat is dry, and the words barely come out.

"Do you need to go to the hospital?" he asks.

"No," I say.

"Do you need a ride into town?"

"Yes."

"Where're you headed?" he asks.

"Brookings," I say.

"That's not far. I can take you there. We'll call a tow truck in town, no reception out here."

"OK," I say.

I start to walk toward his car, but this time he stops me. "We need to move your car out of the road," he says. I release the emergency brake, put the car in neutral and we push the car closer to the shoulder without pushing it off the slope. I grab my suitcase and put it in his trunk.

He walks to his passenger door, opens it for me, and I sit down. The car is warm inside, and it soothes me, removing the edges of chill. He gets inside and starts to drive.

"So, you don't know what you hit?" he asks.

"No," I say.

"People hit stuff all the time around here. Gotta be careful driving around here at night. Things bigger than what you hit, like deer or moose."

There is a sensation in my hand. I forgot that I have been holding onto something. It is Doug's collar, his name clearly printed on the tags.

I catch the man looking at me and the collar. He looks back to the road. We do not talk for the rest of the ride.

<u>2.5</u>

Queen Amarantha rode her steed hard into battle. Her speed and sturdiness projected valor and courage, and it supplied her host with strength to follow their warrior queen. They rode swiftly from her palace, down the ravine and across the grassy plane into the valley below. There was a sweetness to the wind as it crossed her face and combed her thick elegant braid. Trumpets and drums sounded behind her, calling for triumph and glory.

The queen and her army approached the thunder cloud. Thick bolts of lightning struck the ground, tearing through grass and dirt and lighting it with fire. She saw the opposing forces. They were small in number, but they were still enemies.

They did not ride any beast, but they ran with speed and fury to meet Amarantha and her army. They were the shape of humans, but they wore no clothes. They were featureless, faceless and black as night. It was an army of the entity she met when she first arrived in this place, the one around which her spirit wrapped, the one which inhabited a part of her or she it.

Queen Amarantha stood on her steed as it sped toward the battle. She grabbed a shaft from her quiver and nocked an arrow. She inhaled and released. The arrow arced across the sky and into the heart of the thundercloud. The red and purple lights in the cloud flickered and went out. The lightning, too, strobed and struck only a few more times but ceased. The cloud lowered and plowed nose first into the ground, breaking apart on impact. The army of humanoids stumbled, broke rank and watched as the cloud dissipated into fragments and mist.

Queen Amarantha slowed her steed. She sensed victory. She motioned for one of her commanders to approach. "Take them as prisoners," she said, pointing to the motionless enemy army. "If they fight, kill them. If they surrender, do not resist them." She stayed the rear as her host surrounded the enemy. One long rope was tied around their hands and necks, binding them in a single-file line.

The prisoners, about fifty, were marched to the palace dungeon. As they passed Queen Amarantha, she felt their gaze though they had no features with which to stare. One of her soldiers quickly ran to her. "My queen," it said, "there is something wrong."

The soldier led her to the place of the capture. On the ground writhed one of her soldiers with seizures and tremors. He groaned and clenched his teeth in pain. He was breaking apart, chipping away, losing his life and color and turning to blackness and ashes.

"What happened?" the queen asked.

"An enemy harmed him," replied the soldier.

"How?" asked the queen.

"By touching him," said the soldier.

Queen Amarantha tried to kneel and examine the dying soldier, but those around her held her back. "You must not touch him," said the soldier, "or it may spread to you."

"Then what can be done?" she asked.

"Nothing. He is beyond aid. He will leave this world and we will never see him again."

Queen Amarantha wept from love and pity and confusion. The dying soldier broke to black pieces. For the first time in the history of this world, something died and would not return.

#

Amarantha returned to her palace from the battle. The children were out and whispered hushed curiosities. The queen passed them and entered her library. She sat and considered how to handle the prisoners.

She reflected on execution, if that was necessary or even possible. Or maybe building a city-prison to quarantine them. It was clear they intended to charge into her palace. But was it for violence and destruction? Was it for power? Or something else altogether?

The thundercloud was a war machine, she concluded, manufactured by these entities. But where did they come from? Were there more of them? What relation did they have to this world imbued with the eternal attributes of beauty, courage and justice?

She decided to attempt to question the prisoners, which she would do on her own. She did not want to risk any of her citizens coming into contact with one of them. She stood and exited the library.

When she opened the door, there was the soldier from before. "Where are the prisoners?"

"In the dungeon."

"And are there any more casualties?"

"No. The prisoners are secured."

"Good. Bring me to them."

"Yes, my queen, but—" the soldier hesitated.

"Yes?" asked Queen Amarantha.

"One of them escaped," said the soldier.

"Grab a few of our best men and come with me," said the queen, reaching for her armor and weapon.

<u>3</u>

It is morning. I have been lying awake in bed for the last two hours. I do not need to open the curtains to know that it is overcast outside and that the sun cannot break through the clouds. The patter of cold rain hits the window, and the room is dark enough to sleep in, were I able to sleep.

I sit up, get out of bed and brew coffee in the single-cup brewer. I turn the lights on. There is an envelope that some-one slid under the door. The outside reads:

~~*James McDermott*~~
Jamie Williams
There is a letter inside:

Dear Goat-Song *attendee,*

It is our honor to welcome you to this year's production, for which we have the greatest expectations that it will be remembered as our grand achievement. In keeping tradition, we will not release the title of the production until opening night, and only one name of our exclusive worldwide production team and cast will be revealed before then, here in this notice. This year, and for the first time in Goat-Song *history, we wish to honor and express our gratitude to our returning director, Abigail Toussaint of Paris, France, for her hard work and extraordinary vision. It is rare to have someone work on two shows in the same capacity like Mme Toussaint, who directed our previous production of* Flowers and Dragons *in 1962.*
With joyful anticipation we look forward to seeing you.
Sincerely,
Goat-Song
Further instructions: Dress or tuxedo only. Rentals available on night of performance. Arrive one hour in advance of opening curtain. No photography or recording of any kind, violators will be prosecuted.

The letter has gilded edges and silver embroidering in a Celtic design. The paper is rustic, thick and pulpy, but it has the scent of perfume. The font has the glamor of 1920s New York or Paris.

I take a shower and get dressed, and while I'm dressing the phone rings. "Hello?"

"This is the front desk. The mechanic called about your car. He said that you need to go in person to discuss details."

"Thank you. Could you call me a cab?"

"I'll call one right now."

I put the letter on the table next to Doug's collar, finish dressing, prepare coffee to-go and wait in the lobby. The hotel is next to the lake. The hotel is not a chain but local, so the lobby is small, which makes it all the more crowded because a number of the *Goat-Song* attendees are staying here. There are no tourists apart from those who are here for the play. Normally, during this time of year, the only tourists are those in search of changing leaves, though even that brings few tourists: it is hardly worth it up here in late fall, as the trees are close to bare.

The parking lot is plated with wet mulching foliage. Cars pick up and drop off a steady flow of passengers. It is early in the day and the lobby floor is filthy with tracks. I drink coffee and watch the rain drizzle and wonder why it is hard to wake up when the sun is not out.

The taxi arrives and picks me up. The driver unbuckles, stretches behind the passenger seat and opens the rear passenger door from the inside, a preemptive move ensuring no one sits in the front. I push my way through a crowd, making sure one of these vultures does not take this taxi.

I climb in. The driver looks at me in the rearview mirror. "Loren's Auto," I say, "It's at—"

"I know where it is," she says and she puts the car in gear and drives.

We pull onto the state highway that heads toward downtown and I take in Brookings, seeing it for the first time in daylight. I'm familiar with this area, but I have not been to Brookings before. The lake next to the hotel is wider than it seemed last night. Hills run around the lake, and the mountains loom over all. There are cabins and lodges on the lake that are in transition, some empty and some alight with their winter owners. The year-round population of the town is probably around two thousand. The town seems sleepy and grumpy, its routine annual energy spent on summer tourists, and now, with *Goat-Song*, it is forced beyond its time of hibernation like a child past its bedtime.

There is a building fitted in a valley among the lake hills. I nearly miss it because its architecture molds seamlessly into the flow of the valleys and trees. It is hard to tell how large it is from here, but it appears monstrous.

"What is that?" I ask the driver, pointing to the structure.

"That's the theater," she says. "Took them the last twenty-five years to finish it."

"Finish it?"

"The theater burned down at the last *Goat-Song*. The town nearly forced them to relocate but didn't."

"Why not?"

"They bought the city off."

Everything except driving taxis is a conspiracy with taxi drivers.

"The new theater is impressive," I say.

"They brought in most of the materials from Ottawa and Montreal. Laborers were flown in from Japan. The architect was from Germany. Hard to get Americans to do that kind of workmanship anymore. No one knows a trade here. All they want to do is make videos for their channels. Everyone's obsessed with their platforms."

"But no one knows how to build one," I say. She eyes me suspiciously, unsure if I'm agreeing with her or mocking her. I do not reassure her one way or the other.

We turn onto the main road. There are souvenir shops and restaurants that are unseasonably populated. The tourists are bundled from the cold, but they are dressed in a fashion and elegance that marks them as upper-class outsiders.

"What caused the fire?" I ask.

"They did," she says.

"Electrical?"

"No. It was part of the act."

I think about this and wait to see if she will explain. I ask, "And it got out of hand?"

"No," she says. She swallows her impatience. "It wasn't just the fire that was part of the act. Burning down the theater was part of the act."

She pulls into Loren's Auto and stops the car. "I like you," she says, "so let me give you some advice."

"OK."

"When you go to the play, sit near the back. And wear good running shoes."

#

There is a kid at the desk, probably about twenty, on the computer. He sees me walk in. "I'm clocking out for lunch," he says to me before I have a chance to speak, "let me get Loren for you." The kid walks into the garage, speaks to Loren, points to me, walks to his truck and drives away.

Loren's is both an auto repair and a personal hunting and fishing trophy palace. Aging framed pictures of big game catches spot the wall. The pictures are close to thirty years old. There is a stuffed elk's head over the front desk and a mounted salmon above the two-chair waiting area.

Loren walks to the front desk from the garage, wiping grease off his hands, which are missing a few digits. He walks with a limp and his eyes warn me against being caught staring at his gait. The pictures on the wall are Loren in his youth. It is obvious his endeavors were a hunt for something more. By his looks, he either never found what he was searching for, or he forgot about the hunt altogether.

"Jamie?" he asks.

"Yes."

He motions for me to follow him as he limps into the garage. "You're not gonna like it," he says. He leads me through the garage and to a car lot behind the shop. The rain is now a light mist. There, sitting on the grass, is my car. There is about three-fourths of it remaining if you measure it sideways, passenger-driver. The passenger's side appears fire-damaged, black and brittle, with flecks of black layers shedding onto the grass.

"What happened?" I ask.

"Jack towed it in last night. I was here working late. Jack and I noticed this," he points to the diseased area of the car. "There was only a little bit on the roof last night." He brushes his hands on the brittle black metal, which flakes onto the grass, adding to the pile of chips and dust. The black metal smears onto his hands. He subtly winces, and he wipes it off on his jeans. He continues, "Jack was the one you talked to when you called it in. He said you said there wasn't any fire. Right? Only hit something?"

"That's right."

"And this wasn't like this when you left the car?"

"No," I say.

"Well. It seems to be spreading, whatever's going on. There's less of your car now than there was last night." A chunk of the rear crumbles like ice breaking off an iceberg. "See?" he says.

"And you've never seen this before?"

He ignores my question to communicate its stupidity. "I talked to your insurance this morning. It'll be totaled. They should call you any minute, if they haven't already. If there's anything you want out of the car, you should get it now." He leaves me with the car and limps toward the front of the shop. "No shame in crying," he says as he walks away.

There's nothing left inside the car I want badly enough to risk the car caving in on me. I examine the outside. The epicenter is the passenger door area. It is the most damaged. My memory is ablaze with the faceless entity tapping on the window, leaning into the cab and staring at me. I recall the entity placing its hand on the passenger roof as it leaned in.

My phone rings. It is my insurance agent. He explains to me the situation and that my insurance will cover a rental so I can make it home, but I cannot rent the car until the day I return home. We hang up, and I walk to the front of the shop.

Loren comes from the garage and stands at the register. He types on the computer and writes out a retail document in pen. "I'll only charge you for the tow," he says, and he gives me the document. Out the window, I see the kid park his truck, returning from his lunch break. I reach for my wallet but stop as Loren hunches in sudden agony. He can barely moan, and he catches himself on the counter.

"What's wrong?" I ask. I come around to help him, but he waves me away. His hand is black, and the blackness spreads up his arm. Black lines rise up his neck, and his hand crumbles like dry rot. He takes two steps and falls face first onto the tile, hitting the floor with the sound and consistency of ash. All that is left of him is a human-shaped pile of charcoal shavings.

The kid walks into the shop. He says to me, "Is someone helping you?" He walks around the desk to clock-in on the computer.

"I—" is all I get out before he sees what is left of Loren.

"You've gotta be kidding me," he says to himself, not knowing that the pile of ash is his boss. The kid walks to a small closet, grabs a vacuum and cleans up Loren's ashes. "Sorry," he says to me over the sound of the vacuum, "no one else cleans up around here."

3.5

Queen Amarantha and five of her best soldiers followed the escaped prisoner's trail. They brought long weapons to fight with distance and sheltering supplies in case the journey lasted into the night. The trail of the enemy consisted of flattened or broken grass, scents and scorchings along the ground—the blackness that spread from the prisoner's touch. But these marks did not spread in a recognizable pattern. Sometimes, there were tracks in the ground from which blackness disseminated, or the tips of shrubs ruined by touch and the blight dripping to their rotting roots. Other times, there were trampled and swayed plants as if the prisoner's touch had no effect. The path, at first, was not difficult to follow, but the randomness of the decay was disconcerting. The prisoner was intelligent and capable, secreting as much or as little poison at will and manipulating the poison's advance.

The queen and her soldiers, steedless and on-foot, ran across the valley over which her palace faced. The trail of the prisoner vanished into a field of decay as they came to the battlefield. Queen Amarantha's heart dropped. The ground of the battlefield—moments ago fresh and alive with the substance of this world—was fragile with blackness and barren. Fissures, riven earth, cliffs pulling deep into the swirling abyss beneath the plane. The crumbling rot reached for her palace. The war machine was not defeated. It was a success long before she reached it. It was a cloud of those creature's poison. Whether she shot it down over the valley or the cloud made its way to her palace, it did not matter. It did the work they intended it to do.

Queen Amarantha crouched. "I have failed," she said to her soldiers. "They will destroy this world. They not only turn to dust our creatures who touch them. It is worse than I feared. They turn all material they desire to this blackness. And they are imprisoned in the palace. There is no prison that can hold them."

"My queen," said one of her soldiers, "do not forget you have a legion at the palace. They can fight in your absence. Let me return to carry word of the immediate execution of the prisoners, if execution is possible. You and the others continue the search for the prisoner. We know what waits for us at the palace. We need you to search out what further dangers lie ahead."

"You speak wise words," she said to her soldier. She stood and regained her confidence. "Go, and do as you say. But guard the little ones above all, even the palace."

But when the queen turned to the palace, she saw it crumbling. The blackness spread down the valley toward her. They were caught between the spreading of the battlefield to the palace and the spreading of the palace to the battlefield. She watched as the hill on which her great house stood crumbled and all that it upheld fell into the great swirl beneath the plane. Her subjects fled in panic and terror down the hill and into the valley but were overtaken as the ground gave way and they dropped into the abyss. There were winged creatures, mourning and lamenting, circling the chasm in which fell her queendom.

An angelic creature flew to Queen Amarantha and said, "Your house and all that dwelt in it, living and not, are gone."

"What of the prisoners?" she asked.

"They have fallen, not one is left. As have the little ones. Only we who fly escaped. The rest have perished."

The soldiers laid their weapons and wept. Their world, seen and unseen, homes and hopes, all they built and all they loved, their history and future, swept away at the foundations. They looked to their queen for answers, and they feared she had none.

A mix of sadness, hopelessness and determination came over Queen Amarantha. "We will rebuild," she said. "We will regain our world and construct an empire of peace and prosperity. But there is at least one left, the prisoner who escaped. It must be stopped before it continues this path of destruction. And if there are more like it, we must cast them into the abyss." On hearing this, her soldiers picked up their weapons.

"Return," she said to the angelic creature, "and instruct those who can fight to follow us. The prisoner's trail leads there," and she pointed across the battlefield to the Amethyst Forest.

4

The days are shortening, and the sun is setting. I walk along the main strip to do research on those attending *Goat-Song* while the people are out in what is left of the daylight. A few stop to talk but most do not want to do an interview. Those who participate have little knowledge about the event. I have yet to see any children.

"Jamie!"

Someone catches my attention. Across the street are Tom and Maddie, the Californians with the motorhome. Tom is waiving at me, motioning for me to cross the street. Maddie is so small and encased in winter apparel that she looks like a cloth doll brought to life. I cross the street to greet them.

"Heya, Jamie, didn't expect you to be here," says Tom. The bundle of clothes where Maddie's head is supposed to be nods. "How did you get tickets to *Goat-Song?*"

He is not acknowledging what happened and, until I learn more from them, I see no reason to bring it up. "I'm reviewing it for a paper," I say.

"Oh-ho, this is work for you," he says. "You're not on vacation like most of us."

"That's true. You know anything about the play?"

"The play? No, we don't know what they're performing this time. But Maddie here is a *Goat-Song* legacy. Her mother, grandmother and great-grandmother combined attended the last two productions. This will make number three for her family."

"Really?" I ask.

Maddie lowers the scarf wrapped around her face so that her mouth is visible. "Yes," she says.

"What were the last productions?" I ask in the general direction of her eyes, which I cannot see.

Maddie's mouth half-curls. "Um, one was *The King's Angel* and the last was *Flowers and Dragons.*"

"That's when the theater burned down?" I ask. Maddie places her scarf over her mouth.

"Go inside, I'll be right in," Tom says to Maddie. She walks into a nearby restaurant. Tom, out of some primeval sense of husbandly protection, steps between me and the restaurant into which his wife enters. He speaks softly, "I know you don't mean anything. Tread lightly."

"I don't understand."

"Maddie's mother died in the fire."

"Died?" I say. "I thought it was part of the show."

"That's—" He stops. He thinks carefully about what to say next. "That's what some people say. That's unofficially true. But *Goat-Song* claims it was an accident."

"So did they intend to kill Maddie's mother?"

"They didn't intend to kill her. But they intended to burn the building down. Everyone knows it but no one will admit it."

"Was anyone else hurt?"

"Maddie's grandmother says a few were. There is possibly one other death, and I think that's more than rumor."

"Do you know the name of the other?"

"Usui," he says. "Japanese family. They're legacies, too, that's how we know them. There aren't many legacies. They don't talk much, but something about the last show shook them up. But they're devoted to the show. They even helped rebuild the new theater."

"Even though one of them died?"

"Yeah," he says.

"Who are the other legacies?"

"Listen, Jamie—"

I recognize this immediately: the question line. It is different for everyone, but everyone has one. I do not know why answering questions in succession increases our suspicions and makes us uncomfortable, but it does. I am one question away from the line between friend and enemy. I do not want to push it yet with Tom and Maddie.

"Why don't you go enjoy your meal," I say. "Tell Maddie I'm sorry. I didn't mean anything by it."

Tom's face brightens a bit. "Thanks. We'll see you around," he says. All too happy to be free, he walks into the restaurant.

#

There are groups walking toward the lake, and I follow them. The main strip is about half a mile from the water. The air becomes crisp, and the closer I get to the water, the icier the air becomes.

There is an unexpected anticipation in the air, the people buzz with chatter and laughter and excitement. Some walk faster than me, half pushing me aside as they pass. There are now hundreds of people walking down the middle of the street. Their talk goes like this:

"What do you think they'll do this year?"

"Turn your flash off, you don't want to get caught."

"I hear it's unlike anything they've done before."

"Hurry, it'll start soon."

The crowd gathers along the edges of the water. The sun is beneath the horizon, prematurely setting, as is the case this time of year, and it is almost dark. The street lights are not lit, and there are extinguished lamps lining the shoreline.

I walk to the edge of the water. The water is trembling. The lights dim in the cabins across the lake. The last blue of sunset wavers and fades. Only the glow of the moon reflected in the lake illumines our surroundings.

A single light along the shoreline comes alive. Then another. One by one they shine. The crowd is silent, watching, waiting. The lights turn on and off in a pattern, flickering, dancing. It is amusing at first, like twinkling Christmas lights. And then it all stops.

One person claps half-heartedly, unsure if they should or not. "Is that it?" someone asks. We wait for about five minutes. The crowd begins to disperse.

"Look!" someone says.

The reflection of the lake changes color. It transitions slowly at first, from the black night sky, until it brightens, reflecting a colorful afternoon sky. And in the water's reflection emerge three suns over the mountains: one green, one blue and one purple. It is an enchanting and unreal sight. Our faces glow with the false reflection in the lake.

There is something in me that moves me to do what I do next. I bend down, cup my hands and scoop some of the lake water. To my shock, and to the shock of those around me, the water in my hands continues to reflect the same well-lit colored sky. Others do the same, and in a moment these wealthy social elite are transformed into mesmerized children enjoying something they have not experienced in years: wonder.

The three suns reflected in the water flicker in a dance, mimicking the lights along the shore and revealing the lamp dance for what it was: an appetizer and a misleading imitation of this, the true magnificence. The suns orbit each other, pulse and shimmer, and the heart of everyone watching in this moment belongs to these gods of wonder.

As the mystery rejuvenates me with life, and like a balloon about to burst I think that I cannot bear anymore, the unthinkable happens: color seeps into the night sky, the true night sky, not that reflected on the water. We all gaze upward, and like paint spreading from behind the mountains, pastels reach across the arc of the sky. The stars fade and the three suns rise over the horizon, over the mountains, orbiting, shimmering, pulsing, and the town is alive with colorful daylight. Their heat pierces the night's cold. I stare at my hands which somehow feel the warmth emitted from the illusion in the sky.

No one speaks. What can words express that the eyes cannot see at this moment? I do not know whether to be amazed or horrified. How are they doing this? What kind of technology drives this? The illusion is so real that I wonder for one moment if Earth will be knocked out of its orbit. And to call it an illusion seems unfair. It is not a hallucination; we all see it. It is not a cheap trick; the entire town is as it was during mid-afternoon. There is a great power in this act, one that I do not understand, and even after all that has happened over the last few days, it is only now, under this inescapable and unnatural daylight, that I seriously consider whether I am in over my head, and whether I have already been overtaken.

The suns retreat into the universe. The sky darkens from the horizon to the zenith. The stars are returned to us by those wielding power over the heavens, and the cold from the lake returns. The lights along the shore and street lamps come on, and the crowd erupts into applause and laughter. A woman standing next to me claps and smiles. She is well dressed and is probably in her sixties, possibly pushing seventy. We catch each other's eyes. We do not know each other but that does not matter. We have the camaraderie of shared experience. She says to me, "I can't wait to see what they do tomorrow night." She stops clapping and grabs her purse from the ground.

"They're doing more?"

"Sure. They go all out the night before the play. At least, that's the way it's been traditionally. I don't know how they're going to outdo what they did tonight."

"I don't know how they *did* what they did tonight," I say.

She playfully bats my shoulder. "Hush," she says, "or you'll spoil all the fun. You can't enjoy a performance until you forget you're watching one."

She seems knowledgeable about what is going on, so I ask her, "How well do you know *Goat-Song*?"

"If you knew what I knew, you'd know that no one knows *Goat-Song* well," she says.

"But you know more than I do."

She thinks this over. "I know enough about *Goat-Song* that when I describe it I sound like a Zen master telling *koans*. And like a Zen master, you may have a hard time telling if I know what I'm talking about or if I'm faking."

"You have some free time tonight?" I ask.

She smiles. "I'm staying at the Moose Lodge just up the road. There's a bar in the lobby, and we can talk there. But let's call a taxi. I don't want to walk in the cold."

We walk to the road. There is a line of taxis waiting. We get into the backseat and give the driver our destination, and he drives.

"My name's Jamie," I say. "I didn't catch your name."

"Of course, you didn't *catch* it," she says, "My name isn't something I drop or throw. It's too precious a thing for that."

There is a moment of silence between us.

"I give it," she says. She looks me in the eyes. "My name is Kate."

#

The Moose Lodge is a high-class hotel. The decor is that of a hunting lodge, the feel is that of a clubhouse and the layout is that of a saloon. The hotel is made of wood, with vaulted ceilings and large rugs and mounted animal heads. The first floor is large and open. There is a massive two-sided stone fireplace and an open dining area with tables and a bar. There are stairs to the second floor, which overhangs the dining area, and the rooms on the second floor are the guests' rooms.

When we enter, I feel immediately out of place—underdressed, undergroomed, under-classed. I do not hesitate much but enough that Kate notices. She loops her arm around mine and carries me through the dining area and to the bar. The lobby is half-full of customers indulging in late-evening snacks and drinks and conversation.

We sit down, and she says, "Don't worry, these people bleed if you cut them, just like you. Except their blood is blue. And it's probably worth more than yours."

"I didn't see this place," I say.

"What do you mean?"

"When I was looking into hotels in the area to stay in, this place didn't come up."

"Of course not," she snorts, "it's been booked years in advance. You practically have to be a legacy to get a room here. Most families book them for the next generation while they're here. That's what my father did for me, and yesterday I booked my grandson's room for the next *Goat-Song* when he's old enough."

The bartender walks to us. "Good evening, Ms. Kate. Dry martini, straight with an olive?"

"Please," she says.

"And for you sir?"

"I'll have the same," I say.

Kate looks surprised. "You like martinis?"

"They're fine."

"I don't often think of people your age and younger drinking martinis. But maybe I'm out of touch. So, what do you want to know, Jamie?" She rolls my name around her mouth like a lollipop, and I can almost hear it click against the inside of her teeth.

The bartender gives us our drinks. We each take large drinks. She watches me carefully to see if I wince, to see if I pass the test.

"Do you know the Usui family?" I ask.

"Yes. They're good friends of mine. Our parents were close and us kids became close, too."

"How do I get in touch with them?"

"That's a good question. They don't stay at the lodge. They have their own home in the mountains. They rarely come into town when they visit, and I doubt they will come into town before the show."

I don't speak right away, but I consider this. "You visit Brookings even apart from the official production? Since you played together as kids, I mean."

"Oh yes. Every few years I visit Brookings. *Goat-Song* is meaningful, and location is essential to meaning, like Mecca or Jerusalem or Rome or Heaven. Too much of a thing's meaning is lost when you cannot point in its direction."

"Is that how you think of *Goat-Song*? In a religious way?"

"We'll get to that later," she says. "You were asking about the Usui family."

I take a drink. "How can I find the Usui home?" I ask.

"I don't guarantee they'll speak to you. It doesn't hurt to try, they're hospitable and inviting. If you go up this road about a mile and a half past this lodge, it starts to ascend into the mountains. You'll come to a gate on your right. The road beyond the gate leads to their house. There's a callbox, and you can talk to them there."

Kate takes a drink. "My throat is parched," she says, "you got me talking and I'm not used to it." Kate is excited with the interview. "What's next?"

"How long has *Goat-Song* been in production?"

"You don't know? You are starved of data, aren't you?" She is happy with having the upper hand in this. "*Goat-Song* has been in production for three hundred years. Exactly three hundred years. This is the fifth anniversary."

"Fifth anniversary? I didn't know that."

"That's probably because *Goat-Song* doesn't advertise anything. It's all word-of-mouth. That's the way they do it, and that's the way we like it. We adore a level of improvisation."

"What do you mean?" I ask.

"For example, how did you come across the show at the lake tonight?"

"I saw groups of people walking to the lake and followed them."

"So, no one told you about it in advance?"

"No."

"Good. That's the way it's supposed to be. *Goat-Song* doesn't tell you anything. It's a discovery."

I think about this for one moment. It is true that it seemed as if I were stumbling across the show. "But if it's designed to construct discovery, then it's not real discovery," I say.

"That's part of the confines of art, but that does not undo the experience. It is an experience of discovery nonetheless, whether it's artificial or organic. There is reality, and then there are the fantasies of reality in our minds, and then, on rare occasions, there are bridges marrying the two. There is a horse in the world, and a unicorn in your mind, and, who knows, one day you may stumble across a real unicorn."

"And *Goat-Song* is that bridge?"

"No. *Goat-Song* is bigger than that. They construct your reality, and your fantasy, and your bridge, and marry them, all the while convincing you it's happening naturally. And who's to say it isn't?"

We pause to drink.

"Are you part of the production team? Or are you only here to watch?"

"No," she says, "anyone who is part of production is at the theater, and they are not allowed to leave or to come into contact with you or me before the play. There are strict rules about that. But I wouldn't say I'm here only to watch, because that sounds like I'm an observer. No one is merely an observer, as you should have learned after tonight."

"How so?"

"Were you not the one who bent down and filled your hands with water? Were you not the one who filled yourself and those around you, including me, with awe as the water in your hand carried the reflection? You were a designated contributor as much as you were an observer. No one else scooped the water."

Kate finishes her drink.

"Designated? You're saying they designed tonight's performance knowing someone was going to do that?" I ask.

She shakes her head. "Not someone. You."

I finish my drink. "Can you prove it?"

"No. But neither can you."

The bartender checks in on us. "Another drink?"

"No, thank you," she says, answering for the both of us.

She continues speaking to me, "My father attended *Goat-Song*'s last production, and it's hard to express how much he changed afterward. I was just a child." She doesn't continue the thought. She rubs the countertop absentmindedly with her finger.

"Actually," she says to the bartender, "bring us two more." He nods. She does not speak, waiting for her martini. When he sets them before us, she takes a big drink.

"How did he change?" I ask, not wanting to lose the momentum of the conversation.

Kate closes her eyes. A flush of red enters her cheeks. "It was like he could see through walls. That's the way my mother described it. I've not thought of a better way of putting it. Imagine you always knew what was on the other side of the wall, any kind of wall, whether literal walls or immaterial walls. He saw through people, through their self-deceptions, through their ulterior motives. On one hand, you would have a greater sense of satisfaction, life would make more sense, and on the other hand you would feel disconnected from everyone, no one else could see what you see, understand what you understand. No one would want to believe that you could see through them. Those who are self-deceived violently defend their walls of self-deception while the rest do not believe it exists. I learned an important lesson from what happened to my father. In the land of the blind, the one-eyed-man is not king. He is a myth-peddler and a beggar. Sight is so beyond them, so fantastic, that telling them about it provokes ridicule and unbelief. That was my father. He saw through walls while others stared at them. He had a joyful melancholy, perpetually unsatisfied by an overdose of satisfaction."

"Zen *koans*," I say.

She takes a long drink that finishes the glass. "If you're interested in learning about *Goat-Song* from those who have grown up with it, you have to view it like we do. Brookings is our Rome, our Jerusalem. This is less about a play and more about a way of life, a religion, like Burning Man or a total solar eclipse. This is an event that many of us have been preparing for our entire lives."

I imitate Kate and empty my glass. When I set the glass down, I realize that we are the only two customers left in the lobby. The hotel staff is cleaning, putting chairs on tables. The bartender is wiping the counter with a damp cloth.

"What time is it?" I ask. "I didn't realize it was getting so late."

"There's one more thing you should know and then we'll call it a night."

"OK," I say.

"My father still lives in me. He passed onto me his secret. He taught me to see through walls."

Kate's face darkens, she is angry, her eyes flash, on the edge of tears, and she adds, "And my mother hated me for it. She couldn't stand the gift my father gave to me. She disowned us, the myth-peddler and his beggar daughter. Do you have kids?"

"No," I say, suddenly defensive of the knowledge of Sarah, and I sense that Kate sees through me.

Kate nods. She unclenches her fist, and her face softens. "Until you understand how deep *Goat-Song* lives in some of us, you'll never understand it. But I can't prove it. My gift, I mean—seeing through walls. And I know how important proof is to you." She stands, "Here I'll say goodnight, Jamie."

"Goodnight, Kate," I say. "Thank you for sharing this with me."

"It's not me who has been sharing with you," she says. She stands, walks to a machine at the wall and presses buttons. She nods goodnight to me and walks upstairs to her room.

Shostakovich comes over the lobby speakers. The machine is a jukebox. And Kate can see through walls.

4.5

The queen and her soldiers came to the edge of the Amethyst Forest. The wind blew and the trees danced with the chattering of precious chimes. To the queen, it seemed as if the trees held long-forgotten secrets and they whispered to each other in delicate crystal voices, alert to her presence, skeptical to her welcome.

There was a trail of ashes leading into the forest. A few trees at the boundary line were infected with the prisoner's black poison. For great lengths, on both sides of the queen and her party, stretched the perimeter of the forest. The edge of the plane, over and beneath which the abyss hung suspended, was not far, and this part of the world of the queen and her subjects consisted of this vast presence of dense purple trees with their crystal leaves and all that hid within. If they were to catch the prisoner, there was no choice but to enter the forest.

"What can we expect to find behind these trees?" asked Queen Amarantha.

"We have never entered the forest," answered one of her soldiers.

"Is it forbidden?" she asked.

"No, my queen, it is not forbidden. But neither do we persuade any to journey here."

"Do you fear the forest?" an angelic figure asked the queen.

"I do not fear the forest," replied the queen. "But there is a presence here that cautions me. These trees are home to more than our escaped enemy. There is something else here, something other than our captive, and it may be into the arms of this other being that our prisoner fled. Do not be afraid, but be on your guard, for here we may find more than our equal."

Queen Amarantha and her party stepped into the forest. The trees rustled. Light filtered through the trees so that the haze and the atmosphere and the shadows glowed shades of purple.

There were animals in the forest, untamed and harboring primal natures. Queen Amarantha had grown so accustomed to the citizens of her queendom who spoke and communicated that the presence of unspeaking wild animals struck her as savagely crude and fearfully unpredictable. There were jewel-crusted birds and rodents with fur like grass. Enormous lizards scuttled across the floor and up the trees, watching the queen and her soldiers, with open mouths and sticky tongues poised for attack.

"My queen!" an angelic creature shouted, and Amarantha turned and saw the prisoner lunging for her, hand outstretched to touch and poison her. The angelic creature dove between the enemy and the queen, intercepting the attack, knocking both the angelic creature and the queen to the ground. The angelic creature suppressed its agony as the poison took hold.

"Attack!" commanded the queen. The prisoner let out a screeching cry. The trees rattled, and the animals fled. The prisoner's speed and strength proved formidable for the queen's soldiers. They fought but were no match, as the prisoner moved spider-like, climbing up and around the trees, tearing the soldiers' weapons from their hands, frantically and swiftly destroying all that it touched. It vaulted from tree to tree, targeting her winged soldiers, striking every one of them down. At the end of the frenzy, Queen Amarantha was left with three unharmed soldiers, the rest dead or dying. The enemy climbed a tree, let out a deathly screech and fled deeper into the Amethyst Forest. She followed it down the vista of trees, designed almost like a labyrinth, the creature twisting to the left, then to the right, then under large roots and finally into a long straightway.

She and her remaining soldiers chased the beast. It leapt across trees, it ran on the ground, desperately infecting all that it touched, scorching the land in a wild and wrathful re-treat.

The queen saw in the distance that the hallway of trees opened into a grassy meadow. The grass was tall and would easily conceal the enemy. "Quickly!" she said, "Before it is lost!"

The queen stopped. She drew an arrow in her bow and she aimed at the prisoner. She inhaled and she released. The prisoner disappeared into the tall grass, but the arrow fol-lowed behind it. There was a sharp yelp as the arrow hit its mark.

The queen stopped the soldiers from walking into the meadow. "You stay behind," she said. "I will see if the pris-oner still lives."

Queen Amarantha walked cautiously to the meadow. She bent back the blades of grass which stood above her head and saw splatters of the black poison. She stepped forward, listening, gently pressing aside handfuls of stems, following the direction of the enemy which moments earlier tumbled through. But she lost the trail.

Agitated, she moved faster through the blades, looking for signs of the prisoner. She listened but heard nothing. She looked up and saw the sky. She was in a glade in the forest, encircled by amethyst trees.

Then Queen Amarantha heard a noise.

It was not the sound of the enemy or her soldiers. It was not anything she had heard in the forest or even in this world. But it was a familiar noise, whirring and beeping. Its connection to her memory captured her attention, and she followed it. She forgot about the injured prisoner and stepped through the meadow until she came to another opening, a circle of shorter grass within the circle of taller grass within the forest. She was in the heart of the Amethyst Forest. And there, at the center, was a machine.

It was a large computer, as tall as her, colored with blinking lights, and connected to it was a chair. Attached to the computer was a grand monitor. Her previous life, her old identity, came back to her with the sight of the machine. She was no longer Queen Amarantha. She was Abby Edwards. And she was scared.

She approached the machine. The computer was technologically advanced, more so than anything she knew. It was a masterwork wielding terrible power. She put her hand on the leather of the chair. The chair was long and reclined at a slight angle. It reminded her of a dentist's chair. But Abby stopped thinking about the chair and the computer and the monitor. Something attacked her from behind.

<u>5</u>

I wake up a couple minutes before my alarm rings. It is bitterly cold in my bedroom. The heat must have gone out sometime in the night. My throat hurts, and it takes no more than that for me to know that today is going to be a long day.

I have not slept much, but there is already not enough time to do the work I planned to do. I worked into the night recording what I know about *Goat-Song* and the experiences I had. I made detailed accounts of my personal thoughts and my conversations with Tom and Maddie and Kate. There is already enough material for multiple articles on the subject, and James may have had a good inclination that this could become a book. Besides the play, which is tomorrow night, and any aftershow material and interviews I'm able to conduct, high on my priority list is to round out my pre-show notes at least with an interview with the Usui family. And I need to return to town for whatever it is that is planned for tonight. Kate indicated that there would be something bigger tonight than last night.

I sit up on the edge of the bed. Dizziness hits me. I carefully stand and feel my way to the thermostat. It reads 70 degrees. There is air coming out of the vent, but it feels cold.

I take a hot shower. It helps for a short amount of time, the steam soothing my skin and my throat, but when the shower is finished, the chill returns. This is not the kind of chill that comes with fever or flu but being outside for too long in winter. But the chill of fever is not far off.

I dress in extra layers, which does not help much. I use my cell phone to call a cab, but I cannot get a signal. I try the phone in the room, but the phone remains silent, and I cannot tell if there is something wrong on my end or the cab company's end. I prepare some coffee to take with me. As I'm about to leave the room, the geometric die next to Doug's collar hums and glows green. I put it in my pocket and walk to the lobby.

The lobby is empty. Yesterday, the place nearly burst, pushed beyond capacity. Now, there are no customers in the lobby. There is no one at reception. I approach the counter and ring the bell to see about fixing the heater and calling a taxi. I wait and no one comes. There are no cars in the parking lot. And then I realize that there is something wrong with how the parking lot appears.

It is cold outside. Not unnaturally cold but end of autumn cold, and the cold feels sharper in my condition. But this is what is wrong: the world is reflecting a purple and pink tint. I step outside and look up. The sun is purple, the same as one of the three suns in last night's performance. Some of the trees are abnormal, too. They appear to have rocks for leaves, like geodes blooming. It is as if I woke up on another planet or inside a painting.

I walk to the road and look up and down it. There is no one. I drink coffee to stay warm, walk back into the lobby and to my bedroom.

I'm feeling worse by the minute. Not only can I not rid my body of this ice, but the faint edge of fever starts in. I keep my clothes on, turn the heat up high and sit on the bed. I empty my pockets on the bed next to me. Sitting becomes exhausting so I lay on my back. I am about to call the day a wash when the bedroom phone rings.

"Hello?"

"Mr. Williams?" The voice is a woman's voice. There is a small hint of an accent but nearly imperceptible.

"Yes."

"This is Murasaki Usui. Our mutual friend Kate contacted me and said you wanted to speak to me."

I sit up and clear my throat and do my best not to sound sick. "Yes. I have a couple questions, if you don't mind answering."

"Of course not," she says, "but not over the phone. Please come to my place. Kate said she told you how to get here."

"I have directions, but I don't—"

"You don't need a ride," she interrupts. "We're not in a hurry. You have all day to walk here without anyone interfering. I made sure of it."

In the pile of pocket contents on the bed next to me, the geometric die glows brightly and chimes loudly.

"Oh," she adds, "bring that with you." She hangs up.

#

I dress as warmly as I can, finish my coffee, prepare a second cup to go and start to walk to the Usui house. There is a distance of about three miles between here and there. Assuming it lies about half a mile past the Moose Lodge, like Kate said.

I exit the motel and walk along the road. There is no heat coming from this sun. It is ornamental and nothing more, a cosmic streetlamp lighting the way. Pink snowflakes drift by, fluttering, light like shredded paper. It is not a heavy snow, but flakes drift every few seconds. The pinks and purples are bewitching, translating me into a cartoon world, a fantasy from which I cannot wake. At a different time, I may not have wanted to wake from this. But it is impossible to enjoy the enchantment with this bone-deep cold and sickness.

I turn the bend and come to the main strip. The lake is down from the shops. The reflection of the sky in the lake is blue, not this purple-pink hue, and the sun in the reflection is the normal yellow sun. I consider jumping into the lake to see if I will surface on the other side of the reflection. If my plan works, though, I may not be able to interview the Usui family. But whether that works or not, I doubt my immune system could handle being drenched in ice water while feeling this sick. The mere consideration of jumping into cold water makes me feel colder and pushes me close to despair. I drink the rest of my coffee, which is lukewarm, and I walk by the lake, through the town and toward the Moose Lodge. There are still no people around.

I pass the main strip and approach the Moose Lodge. The Moose Lodge is not off the road but close to it. There is a short incline from the road onto a gravel pathway that leads to the lodge, and I step up the incline, toward the lodge to ask for help. No lights are on in the lodge, though in this purple-pink hue it is difficult to be certain. I knock on the front door and ring the bell, hoping for a ride or a phone call, or, at the very least, a refill of coffee. There is no answer. Desperately I call out, trying to grab anyone's attention. The snow is falling harder now, not a storm but consistent, and it is cold enough that the snow no longer melts but sticks. There are a couple windows near the front door. I peer in but see nothing. I give up and walk back to the road.

The road bends around the lodge and forks. To the right, it continues as the main highway, but to the left, it turns to gravel and ascends the mountain. Kate said that they live on the mountain's ascent, so I take the gravel road.

As I walk up the road, the air grows colder, the snow falls harder and icicles hang from tree branches. There is wildlife that watches me. Squirrels climb around tree trunks at my approach and deer, ready to sprint, do not take their eyes off me. I am equally cautious of them, unsure what they are like in this world, if it can be called that.

There is a gate on my right. It is an electronic gate. I stumble to it, exhausted, and use the callbox to call the house. There is no answer, but the gate opens. The house is about a quarter of a mile from the gate. The road to the house is paved, but it is covered in snow and this last leg of the climb is the steepest.

I pause halfway up and lean at the waist with my hands on my knees. I cannot tell if I am out of breath or too cold or too sick or some combination of these. There is a rustling sound in the trees in the distance. I look and see the black faceless humanoid. It does not move toward me, but it is watching me. The fear gives me strength, and I stumble as quickly as I can to the house.

I knock frantically on the front door. An elderly Japanese man greets me. He perceives my condition and helps me inside. He helps me remove my shoes. He tries to remove my outer-layers, but I tell him no. He kindly perseveres, and having no energy, I do not fight him. To my surprise, and for the first time since I showered, I truly begin to feel warm.

The warmth returns to my face and my hands. The cold in my bones, the faintness of fever and the soreness of throat all dissipate. I sit on a bench near their front door because the sensation of healing nearly causes me to pass out.

#

"You must be Mr. Williams," the man says. "I am Takuya Usui. Please come in, I will make you some tea. Murasaki will be out shortly."

He leads me to the couch in the living room and helps me sit down. He walks out of the room and to the kitchen. I hear water pouring and then the click of an electric kettle.

The Usui family's house cannot but speak to how well-off they are. The architecture of the house is modern and Western, but the decor is Japanese and it is full of Japanese art. They are clearly art collectors, and all the art is original. Large folding screens are spread across the wall, depicting trees and flowers and birds. There is an alcove in the corner in which sits what looks like small ancient statues, some of them encapsulated in reliquaries. There is an ornate lacquer cupboard containing candles, incense and pictures, presumably, of relatives.

I feel better and rejuvenated just by sitting and warming. I stand and walk around the room, examining the art. On a shelf is a cat with one paw raised, like it is waving at me.

"That is *maneki-neko*," I hear someone say. It is Murasaki. She enters the room from the kitchen carrying two steaming cups of tea. She walks to me and gives one of them to me.

"Thank you," I say. I take a drink. It is green tea, both rich in flavor and light. "What is *maneki-neko*?"

"It's for good luck. They are often at restaurants and are cheap and for decoration. This is a special one. This one is not cheap. But it is missing its good luck charm. See?"

There is a hollow beneath the cat's head. The hollow is small and diamond shaped. Murasaki puts her finger in the hollow and feels it.

"Normally," she says, "*maneki-neko* has a kind of coin as its charm. This one has something more valuable than a coin. But a couple days ago, the charm popped out. It didn't fall to the ground. It popped out of here and went somewhere else."

I grab the geometric die from out of my pocket. It glows and chimes. Murasaki gently takes it from my fingers and inserts it into the hollow.

I'm embarrassed. I try to defend myself, "I don't know how my cat got it, but he did. He coughed it up one day."

Murasaki smiles, "That's OK. There are strange things happening lately. Things that are here find their way over there. I don't know if you have seen the color of outside? Or your *noppera-bo*?"

"What's *noppera-bo*?"

She motions for me to sit on the couch, and I do. She sits on a chair across from me. We both sip the tea.

"It's a ghost from Japanese folklore. A faceless ghost. It takes many shapes. There is rumor of one in these mountains. My great grandfather said he saw him when he was a boy. You saw *noppera-bo*, right?"

I hesitate. "No, I don't think so," I lie, unsure at the moment how wise it is to reveal this.

"Oh," she says. "It surprises me you have not seen it. You must be very lucky. This gem," she points to the green geometric figure, "calls to it when it is taken from *maneki-neko*. Its music is from a different world. Or a different part of our world, depending on how one looks at it."

Takuya enters the room. He speaks to Murasaki in Japanese, and she replies in Japanese. Takuya bows, goes down the hall and to one of the back rooms.

"Takuya is making sure we are comfortable," she explains. "I told him that we will talk now. So, he went to do his hobby."

"What is his hobby?" I ask.

"Birdwatching. He reads books and memorizes their calls. He watches videos online for hours. After *Goat-Song*, we will go to Central Park so he can try to add to his list."

We drink our tea. I finish my cup and set it down. Its warmth and spice strengthen my body and spirit. My mind is alert.

"He also builds set-pieces and props for *Goat-Song*," says Murasaki. "They are quite interesting. We have a nice collection of material used in previous *Goat-Song* plays. Would you like to see some?"

"Yes," I say.

Murasaki stands and walks me down the hall. She opens a door, and we walk down another hall which veers into yet another. Their house is larger and more complex than it appeared from the outside. It is full of paintings and photographs and sculptures. The hall dead-ends but she does not turn into the rooms on either side of us. She pulls back a small rug which is hiding the entrance to an underground passageway. She takes my hand and places it over the perimeter of the passageway and I feel air faintly blowing. She opens the door to our left, which is a utility closet. She takes a hay hook, inserts the hook through the metal loop to the passageway and lifts, revealing a staircase that leads into darkness. "Please, no photographs," she says.

Murasaki enters the passageway first. She disappears as soon as she descends the stairs. I hear a click, and lights turn on. I follow her.

It is a narrow and steep spiral staircase, and I have to watch my head, which descends further underground than I expected. We reach this deep basement and Murasaki, somewhere in the darkness, turns on another light. There are tall paintings and antique tapestries hanging from the ceiling, forming a kind of barrier between the staircase and the rest of the basement. Murasaki is already past them. I maneuver carefully through them, hands above my waist and near my chest like I'm wading through water. After I make my way through, the room opens.

It is a wide finished basement, and it must spread out close to the entirety of the house if not more, eating into the mountainside. There are supporting columns scattered throughout.

"This is where we keep some of our art when it is not on display," she says.

"Which is the art, and which are the props?" I ask.

She looks at me and smiles.

There is one prop I recognize. Displayed along the wall is the dragon I saw in the polaroid from the picture online. "You made this?" I ask.

"Takuya made it," she says. "That was one of the first he made, when he was very young. He is a brilliant craftsman. He learned from his grandfather."

"And Takuya is your husband?" I ask, just to be sure that my hunch was right. But I'm surprised when she does not respond. She pauses and thinks.

"No," she finally says. "Not like you think. We are part of the Usui family. But it is not family like you think. Please do not ask again." She does not look away from me until I nod my head in agreement.

She walks to a long table pushed against the wall. It is an assortment of trinkets. There is no obvious arrangement style, and I cannot tell if it is random or not.

Murasaki picks up a crown. "This," she says, "was from *Goat-Song III*." She shows me the bottom, which has paper with the Roman numeral three. "This was not our best *Goat-Song*, but it was not bad."

"That was *The King's Angel*?" I ask, corroborating what Murasaki says with Maddie.

"Yes," says Murasaki. "But the king was not kingly, and the angel was not angelic." She places the crown on the table, and she grabs a sword displayed on the wall. "This was also from *Goat-Song III*." She holds it out for me.

I take it from her. There is a heft to it I did not expect. "This is a real sword?" I half ask, half exclaim. Murasaki nods. There are reddish brown stains near the tip and along the edge. "Is this blood?"

Murasaki takes the sword from me. "The king was not kingly," she repeats, "and the angel was not angelic." She hangs the sword on the wall. She walks deeper into the basement, and I look closely at the sword as I pass.

"This is from *Goat-Song II*," she says, pulling my attention from the sword. It is a wooden box with a lock on the front. Murasaki sets the box on the floor. She takes the key from the table and opens the box. Inside is a ball and chain. "Do you know about *Goat-Song II*?" she asks. She hands me the ball and chain, which, like the sword, are true in design and weight.

"No."

"It was called *The Escape*. It was about a master and a slave, and it was a metaphor for humankind escaping Hegel's dialectic in history, borrowing from Dante's *Inferno* in its form. The director was a Hegelian, but the writer was anti-Hegel, and their tension made the dialectic all the more believable. That was our best year, I think." She takes the ball and chain from me, puts them in the box, locks it and sets it on the table.

"Why do you say that?" I ask. "That was almost two hundred years ago, you weren't there."

"I have read all the scripts. I have the only remaining copy of the script for *The Escape*. And the props for this are of a higher quality. Masahiro Usui made the props. He was a genius. No one, before or since, matches his quality. Takuya comes close, but he is not Masahiro. It is no shame to be second place to Masahiro. Here is the script." She walks me to the other side of the wall. There is a podium, and on the podium, encased in glass, is an antique book, thin like a novella, and it is opened. The writing is ornate and in Blackletter. The edges contain patterns and drawings like medieval manuscripts.

"All scripts are handmade. The books are handbound and they are handwritten by professional scribes using ink and quill. That year, the play was written and performed in Latin."

"And you read it? You can read Latin?" I ask.

She nods, and she leads me further into the basement. We come to the wall furthest from the spiral staircase, but there is a door that leads further. From floor to ceiling, and from the edge of the door to the wall of the basement, is a single wood carving, an oblong, and encircling the oblong are baroque cherubim. The center is a painting depicting heaven and hell. The painting is an intentional blurring of the two. There is a lush garden surrounded by flames on one side and angels torturing humans in a sun-lit paradise on the other. In the garden are goats with human bodies, bathing joyfully in the flames. In the paradise are singers in anguish as they are tortured.

"This is from the first *Goat-Song*. It is in the rococo style. It established what *Goat-Song* is."

"What is *Goat-Song*?" I ask. "According to this, I mean. I know the word is from the Greek and it means tragedy."

"It is from the Greek in etymology," she explains, "and it is tragedy. I don't know what is more tragic than the sameness of heaven and hell. But etymology is not the same as what it means today. This is what it means. It is the tragic marrying of these ideas. The goat is all that is earthly: violence, corruption, blood, fear, pain. The song is all that is eternal: peace, harmony, love, delight. In *Goat-Song*, the two are brought together as one."

The piece is captivating. It is overwhelming in its scope and magnitude, and I wonder what it is that makes Murasaki see this as subpar to the later designs of Masahiro. But there is something about it that bothers me. At first, I cannot put my finger on it, but then I see it. It is the look of indifference on the faces of the cherubim.

Murasaki opens the door to which the basement dead ends. "We have some extra time," she says, "would you like to see one of the props for this year's performance? Takuya finished it just this morning, so it has not been delivered to the theater yet. He says this is his masterpiece."

"OK," I say.

She steps into the room and turns on the light. I step in and the room is larger than I expected, consistent with the rest of the basement. It is Takuya's workroom. There are tools hanging on the walls and there are workbenches.

"Here it is," she says, walking to the center of the room. She puts her hand on the prop, feeling it, petting it. I lean in to examine it closely.

This is what it is: a reclining chair made of leather, and it is attached by thick cables to a large screen and a tall industrial server rack, the kind made for warehouse databases of large internet companies. The technology is smooth and sleek, a computer more advanced, at least in appearance, than anything I have seen before. The monitor is attached to the computer and the chair. It is paper-thin and the size of a king bed. The entire prop repulses me after looking at the others, which are ornamental, artistic and crafted from another time. This technology seems out of place. Ironically, it seems anachronistic.

"What is it?" I ask.

Murasaki shakes her head. "I don't know. Takuya knows; they tell him since he must build it. But he keeps his secret diligently. He will not tell anyone, not even me, what this is or what he knows of tomorrow's production."

I examine the chair until Murasaki stops me. "I'm sorry, Jamie," she says, "but we will have to end our tour. I sense that it is normal outside again, which means that our time is up. The head of the visual effects artists, his family owes me a favor. And it seems their favor is repaid."

"That's visual effects?" I ask.

"What else would it be? You don't really think the sun is purple or that there are three of them, do you?"

"No," I say, "but to call it visual effects doesn't do it justice."

"That's true," she says. "Think of it like a medieval peasant seeing CGI for the first time. They may call it a kind of puppetry. We call it visual effects now because there is no other word for it yet. But I'm sure someone will think of something."

"Thank you," I say and smile, "this has been an invaluable experience."

She leads me out of the basement, up the spiral stairs, down the halls and to the front door. Takuya comes out of the kitchen with a cup of tea. "Thank you," I say to him, but he does not respond and walks past us.

"Don't mind him," says Murasaki, "his mind is on his hobby. I will tell him you say thank you." She smiles at me and I at her.

I put on my coat and my shoes. Murasaki opens the door. The sky is restored, blue with a yellow sun, the purples and pinks are gone. There is no snow on the ground, and it is unseasonably warm. It is early evening, later than I expected.

"Oh," says Murasaki, "it is nice out. You may not need your coat. I think they are making this year extra special for all of us. The morning was alluring, wasn't it? Goodbye Jamie."

"Wait," I say, until now forgetting why I am here. "I want to ask you about the fire." My tact has left me as I try to undo our parting.

Murasaki is not bothered by the question. "I will say this," she says, and she says it both with kindness and authority. "My daughter was eaten by the flames that year. And it was a large debt that hung over the head of the visual effects artist ever since. But, as I said, the visual effects artist repaid his debt. And I do not like to bring up debts that have been repaid." I nod a thank you. She smiles and waves me off.

As I descend the driveway, I decide to take a picture of their house. I take out my phone and open the camera. Through my phone I see distantly that Murasaki is waving at me, and I think that maybe I can snap a good but uncandid photo of her. I zoom in. A jolt runs through my spine and I'm able to snap a photo before I drop the phone. Murasaki is waving at me. But she has no face.

I pick up the phone and quickly descend the driveway. The gate opens. I rush through it and down the mountain road.

5.5

Abby Edwards woke. She was strapped into the chair with the computer and the screen. She struggled, trying to slip her wrists free, but there were multiple metal clamps up and down her arms and her legs, and there were two large clamps, one around her neck and the other around her waist. A dampness on her face caught the wind as it blew and it stung, and she knew she had cuts and scrapes and patches of blood. She became aware of a throbbing in her head. She remembered the attack.

The black and faceless humanoid, the enemy, walked into her line of sight from behind her. She froze in fear. Then other creatures came into her line of sight. They were her soldiers. They looked at her with malice and derision.

"What is this?" asked Abby.

"It's almost sad," said someone behind her, the voice digitally modified, "how quickly you changed from Abby Edwards to Queen Amarantha. As if you were the protagonist. That's what's wrong with your generation, you all think you're the most important part of the story. I can't imagine what it must have been like to be a royal warrior one minute and a dead young girl the next."

There were noises as of something being constructed behind Abby. The creatures in front of her turned and walked away. Across the meadow she saw the crumbling disease spreading. There was the sound of breaking timber and a patch of trees fell downward into the unseen abyss.

"I don't have time for many questions," the person said, "but we are not unkind and will allow a few. So, think carefully. What would you like to ask?"

Abby regained her composure and her breathing. She looked around her as best as she could, remembering all that had happened up until now. "What is this place?" she asked.

"Excellent question," the person said. "You will be forgiven for thinking that this is a digital world with the computer and the monitor. But it is not. It would have been the work of a true artist to construct this place. But I am not an artist. I am an archeologist. I am an excavator. This world is real. These creatures are real beings. I am responsible for sweeping away that which hides them from our sight. You are the first pedestrian to walk in this world. My crew and I found our way through about ten years ago and no one besides us—which now includes you—have been here."

The Archeologist resumed construction.

Abby thought carefully about her next question. "Am I dead?" asked Abby.

The Archeologist set something down. "I wouldn't say that. But I would not disagree." There was a pause. "Let me put it like this: you're dead but you don't know it yet. There is something in you keeping you alive. You became part of this world when you fused with one of them. For all intents and purposes, you are dead, but this world is keeping you alive."

"I didn't mean to wrap myself around that thing."

The Archeologist laughed. "Mean to? My dear, you don't know the sense of the word. Intentionality is beyond you. You most certainly were meant to. This is how the story goes. You couldn't have stopped it even if you wanted to." The Archeologist fit something together that audibly snapped into place. "There. OK, Abby, you can ask two more questions."

Abby thought carefully. "Is this world really being destroyed?"

"Do you mean by that spreading rot? Yes. But I wouldn't fear falling into that abyss, if I were you. That's how we are both here and there."

Abby did not understand, but she did not want to waste her last question, so she asked, "What will happen to me?"

"You'll see," said the Archeologist. "It's almost time anyway." Abby saw the hand of the Archeologist pressing buttons on the monitor and the computer. The screen faded from black to dim lighting. At first, Abby could not tell what it was she saw on the monitor. But her eyes adjusted, and the shapes made sense and she realized she was looking at herself strapped to the same chair on a stage. And every move she made was made by the Abby on the screen. When she turned her head, at the same instant the counterpart turned her head. When she struggled, the counterpart struggled. She moved in two places at once.

<u>6</u>

I walk to the main strip of town. There are people, unlike earlier, but they are not strolling around or in their cars. They are on the rooftops. And they expect to be up there for a while: they sit in chairs, there are coolers with food and drinks, tables with flowers in vases. The people are alive with laughter, enjoying the warmth and their rooftop picnics. The shops' doors and windows are boarded for protection, like they are prepared for a hurricane.

The reflection of the lake is the world I was in this morning. In it, there are purple and pink hues and snow is falling. It strikes me that the people prefer to talk to each other than to wonder at the lake. The speed at which the remarkable transforms into the mundane is surely evidence of humankind's fallen nature.

"What are you doing down there?" someone calls. "Hurry! Up here!"

There is a small man waving at me, motioning for me to join him on top of a restaurant. "Hurry!" he says again. He disappears and returns with a ladder, which he lowers for me. "Come on!"

I walk to the shop and climb the ladder. There are groups of couples segregated on the rooftop. The man unfolds a chair and pats it, inviting me to sit next to him.

"That was close," he says. He is short and balding with small round glasses. He is European, but I cannot place his accent. To my untrained American ears, it sounds like he speaks three accents at once.

He reaches into a cooler and hands me a bottle of beer. "Thanks," I say.

"This is so exciting," he says. "What were you doing down there? They are about to start."

"What's starting?"

As if my being on the ground did not already give me away, this last question does, and he eyes me curiously and cautiously through his thick lenses. "It is the night before opening," he says. He licks beer foam from his mustache. "This is the last hurrah of the opening ceremony." He takes a drink and sucks beer out of his mustache again. "Are you a journalist?"

"No," I say. He gives me an odd look, and I reconsider what I'm saying. "I'm a legacy, but my father and grandfather wouldn't tell me about it. My grandfather, he especially did not enjoy it. The fire in the theater was not to his taste."

"Ah," says the man, "it is an acquired taste, and many cannot taste it to begin with. You should not be like your grandfather. This is the only culture your country produces. You should be proud." He grabs his bottle of beer. "To your tastes!" he says. "May they be better than your grandfather's." And we take a drink.

"What's your name?" I ask.

"Mateo," he says. He points his bottle at me.

"Jamie," I say. "What's with the suitcase?" I ask.

Mateo looks at the packed suitcase next to his chair and then to me. I cannot decipher the look on his face, but it is something like *What is wrong with you?* and *You poor fool.* Before he answers, there is a small quake, and we both lean forward, gripping the armrests of our chairs. Mateo looks at me and smiles, and his smile smears across his face like runny cheese.

The setting sun dims early, like the dimming of lights before a show, and the people, true theater folk, hush, conditioned to quiet at fading lights.

In the dull lighting, the purple and pink hues of the lake glow spectacularly. The water ripples. There is something large swimming in the water.

A serpent breaks the surface, terrible and angry. It lashes and surveys us. It snaps at a rooftop near the water's edge, picking up someone in its mouth and swallowing them.

I stand out of instinct, ready to run, but Mateo puts his hand on my leg, sitting me down. He looks at me and shakes his head. "It is an act," he says, "this is all in fun." He taps my knee a couple of times to settle me down as if I were a dog. I think of the theater fire and of Murasaki's sword with the blood on it and wonder how fine a line there is between an act and danger in this place.

The serpent swims to the middle of the lake in the distance and dives under the water, shifting from this world into the world of the reflection of the water, into the world of purple and pink hues and snow. What was a water serpent here is now a sky serpent or a dragon in the reflection, swimming or flying toward the purple sun. It swims through the sun, piercing it, and out of the sun first dribbles then flows a purple liquid. The liquid falls into the lake. And the lake, our lake, turns purple and rises.

It is no longer only me but many of us stand and watch as the water level rises. The lake creeps up the shoreline and makes its way to the main road. Soon the road is underwater, and the water level advances upon the shops. The flooding levels off at the height of the single-story roofs. The town is underwater, and we are stuck on the rooftops.

Mateo claps his hands in satisfaction. "Wow," he says. He points to his suitcase and says, "Would you like to borrow a change of clothes for tomorrow night?" He looks at me and I look at him, and now that we are both standing I see that the top of his head is at my chest.

The chatter of the crowd grows, and it catches the attention of both Mateo and me. We look to the lake. Drifting across the lake is the theater. The theater floats with a life of its own to the center of the lake and stops, finding its place.

The theater flashes, blue and green hues display the building as the masterpiece it is. It is a bold and marvelous work of architecture. Searchlights dance across the sky at the entrance. It is massive, like a cruise ship, and it is lit brightly enough that the stars in the sky hide their faces. A paved pathway the width of a street rises from beneath the water, as a pier that leads from the theater toward the submerged downtown Brookings.

The doors to the theater open. What appears to be the cast files out in smooth austerity, dressed ornately, like princes and princesses of 19th-century Europe. There are hundreds of them. They approach us on the pathway, crossing the lake, and they stop halfway between us and the theater. Then an angelic-like being emerges from the theater, tall, maybe three times the size of a human, with white feathered wings and a flaming sword. It is strikingly real. There is no indication that this is a puppet or a work of robotics. It walks toward us and sets its feet firmly at the halfway mark. It raises the sword, warning us from entering, guarding the theater. The princes and princesses return to the theater and file inside. The sight is truly awesome: a heavenly guardian with its flaming sword, the theater behind it, the flooded town whose reflection is of another world. I see for the first time that the serpent swims in the reflection, trapped in the world beneath the surface.

"Now we wait," says Mateo. "Do you want to stay at my place tonight?" His runny smile runs again, and he unfolds a cot for himself and a sleeping bag for me.

I look at the sky.

"Don't worry about that," he says. "The sun is out for the night. And I wouldn't try to cross the lake before tomorrow if I were you," and he points to the angel.

Part III

I wake up. There is a pre-dawn grey light, but it feels later. I check my phone for maybe the twentieth time over the course of the night. and it reads 9:00am. Startled, I sit up, wondering why it is still so dark this late into the morning. Some are awake on the rooftops, but others are asleep. There is dew on the sleeping bag, and my hair is wet. It is not cold. The air is still and tepid.

I stand and try to brush some wrinkles out of my clothes. The town remains flooded. My belongings and my clothes for this evening are at the hotel, which I will only be able to get to by boat—assuming my things have not been ruined by the water.

The angelic guardian stands alert with its flaming sword. It appears not to have moved throughout the night. The water continues to reflect the world of purple and pink hues with falling snow. The serpent is there, too, swimming or flying in the reflection.

Mateo squirms on his cot. He reaches for his glasses and sits up. "What time is it?" he asks.

"Nine," I say.

"It's still dark," he says. "And it's warm."

"Yes."

"That was kind of them," he says.

"What do you mean?"

"To make us sleep outside but keep it comfortable for us."

"You think they did this?" I ask, not fully knowing whom I am referencing.

"Of course, who else would have?" Mateo stands and stretches. "Look," he says, and he waves toward someone behind me.

There is a boat gliding across the water serving food and coffee. The pilot rows to us and drops an anchor fashioned out of a coffee tin filled with concrete. He hands us a small menu that lists about five things.

Mateo orders coffee and a bagel. The pilot looks to me for my order. "Can you bring me to my hotel?" I ask. The pilot nods.

"See you at the show," says Mateo with a mouthful as I climb into the boat.

"I'm at the hotel up the road," I say to the pilot, pointing the direction. He nods and lifts the anchor from the water. He rows and we make our way up the highway.

There is a small puddle of water at the base of the boat that sloshes, and it reflects purple and pink. The smell coming from the boat is rejuvenating. I look at the pilot and put money in his stash and motion toward the coffee. He nods. I pour myself a cup.

The air is warm and humid, perfect for breeding bacteria. It reminds me of a nursing home. A few autumn leaves float on the water.

"The sun won't come out today, will it?" I ask. He does not answer. I study the sky and see from the position of the lighting that the sun is high in the sky, but it is covered by this greyness that dilutes it.

We arrive at the hotel. As with the other buildings, the first floor is submerged, so there is no entering through the lobby. "That's my window," I say, and he maneuvers us toward it. He drops the anchor and steadies me as I stand uneasily in the boat and open the window.

"Can you pick me up for the performance this evening?" I ask. He nods. I try to give him some money, but he refuses. He pulls up his anchor and rows back to town.

My room is torn to pieces. Someone searched my things. The suitcase is disemboweled, clothes are strewn across the bed. The lights are flickering, the power surging through the room. But my laptop is on, running a program that I do not recognize, a black screen with code rapidly writing and changing. This is what is using up the power in the room.

The bathroom light strobes on and off, and the door is shut. I search the room for something to use as a weapon. I step silently toward the front door and grab the hotel's iron and then step toward the bathroom. There is a soft voice on the other side of the door. It is unintelligible, but its presence is more troubling than its intelligibility.

I fling the door open with the iron raised to strike. But I drop the iron. Sitting on the edge of the bathtub, sobbing, is my Sarah.

#

"Dad," Sarah says, "they woke me. They found me."

I kneel before her and hug her tightly. She bursts into tears on my shoulder. My shirt becomes wet with her tears. This cannot be an illusion, but I do not know what this is. Her voice is the same, and all the freckles and moles on her arms and neck are the same. I can touch her and feel her. But she flickers as though she were projected by a signal that blips in and out of connection

"It's OK," I say, though I know I have no right to say it. "Sarah, what happened? Who did this?"

"I don't know," she says, ashamed. "Dad, I was dead. I was in another place. But somehow they made a connection between here and there."

"Who?" I ask again.

"People. I don't know who, but living people. Not from where I was but from here. They reached the world of the dead, and they brought me here." She lowers her head and does not look at me. "I'm not supposed to be here. And they're not supposed to be there."

I stand her up and bring her into the bedroom. We sit on the bed. "Do you...are you thirsty?" I ask. She shakes her head. "Hungry?" She shakes her head. She bursts into tears on my shoulder. I am unnaturally whole again. I let her cry for as long as she needs to cry.

I look at her, and I am reminded of the prophet Samuel. King Saul visited the medium at En-dor to summon Samuel from the grave to communicate with Saul. When Samuel appeared, he asked why Saul disturbed Samuel. This is what Sarah is like. She was at peace and outside of our troubles and someone brought her back.

"Sarah," I say. She looks at me. "I love you," I say and then I say something I have wanted to say for years. "I'm sorry I didn't save you."

She smiles and then she flickers for the last time, and my Sarah is somewhere else.

I am relieved for the first time in years. But I am more alone than I have ever been. It was then I realized that my guilt and my anger and my shame had been traveling companions, pushing away the loneliness, hiding me from the world, living entities breathing and throbbing in my soul, and there, in naked isolation, exposed for who I truly am, I cover my face with my hands, for there is nothing else to cover me, and I weep.

#

A tapping at the window wakes me. I open the window, and there is the boat vendor who rowed me to the hotel earlier. He points downward and nods, and he sits in his boat. He is indicating that he will wait for me until I am ready to go to the theater.

The lights in the room no longer strobe, and the screen on my laptop is black. I quickly shower and shave and put on my tuxedo. I look at myself in the mirror, wondering what this evening holds, and wondering if I will see myself in the mirror again.

The man helps me climb into the boat from the window. There are two lanterns lit at the front of the boat. He pulls up his anchor, and we glide along the water toward the theater.

He rows onto the main waterway toward the theater alongside other small boats and canoes that also have lit lanterns, all of different colors, all heading in the same direction. The greyness has lifted, but the sun is set. The sky is clear, and the stars are out. The moon is an odd green color, and it slowly rotates. The moon is a reminder that it is not only the play that belongs to *Goat-Song,* but this place belongs to them, and their power and unknowability looms over my head communicating that I am not a master here but at best an observer and at worst a slave.

The boats on the waterways are motorless, so it is quiet enough to overhear conversations were anyone speaking. But no one speaks, and the faces I look into do not look back. The drag of the boats across the surface of the water is the only noise there is until we reach downtown.

We begin to turn the bend, and there is the theater. It is all that is lit apart from the lanterns. There are no lights on the road. The eye cannot help but be drawn to the theater in all its weight and splendor. When I see it, I become aware of a pressure around my head, and in this darkness it is as if I were in a sensory deprivation tank, the only sound that of wet ripples and the only sight that of a monstrous image floating in black velvet.

As we come around the bend, there are lights along the pier leading to the theater, though the lights in downtown Brookings are snuffed. Boats dock next to the pier, and there are ushers helping patrons out of the boats. In the middle of the pier, the angelic guardian continues to stand, flaming sword in hand, but he does not prevent anyone from passing.

My guide aims the boat toward the pier and closes in alongside it. He drops the anchor and steadies me as I step out of the boat. An usher, a young woman, steadies me as I step onto the pier. I try to give the boat pilot money, but he refuses. I give it to the usher, who gladly accepts it. The boat pilot catches my gaze just long enough for me to notice he is communicating something to me, but not long enough for me to interpret him, and he raises his anchor and drifts into the blackness. The air is thick with this ink, and I realize it is not the air that is the pressure around my head but this absence of light, and all I can see are bobbing and drifting colorful lanterns, though it is impossible to discern depth.

A hand on my back guides me toward the entrance. The young usher smiles at me and then turns to help the next guests who arrive. I pass the angelic guardian. He is enormous and I feel the heat of the flames engulfing the sword.

His skin is an odd blue color, his face is stern and his eyes are black.

I walk toward the theater and see it up close for the first time. Above the entrance there is an elaborate structure that appears to be of wood that is an exact replica of the wooden oblong I saw in the Usui's basement of the first *Goat-Song*. It is the scene depicting heaven and hell and the blurring of the two. Except this is enormous, and it is alive. The cherubim's wings flutter as they circle the perimeter of the image, the people tormented in the garden writhe and scream, though there is no sound, and the people in hell are utterly elated and joyful, dancing and singing. This is not a screen or a hologram but a wooden carving come to life.

There are about ten ushers holding electronic devices and scanning parishioners as they come to the entrance. When I step up, they scan my face, look into the device waiting for the results, and then let me pass through. An usher opens the door for me as I step into the lobby.

The lobby is modeled after the Hall of Mirrors in the Palace of Versailles. The chandeliers look as if they were made of the pink and purple stones I saw blooming on the trees when I walked to the Usui's home, and for all I know, they are. The artwork on the ceiling and along the walls are of past productions. I recognize set pieces Murasaki showed me, such as the box and the ball and chain, and they are woven into the story each scene tells, scenes from past *Goat-Songs*. I also recognize the dragon, though this one is gilded and

gliding above scenes carved into stone. Like the wooden oblong outside, these are living scenes, though they are painted
and carved into stone. We pass by these as we make our way
to the auditorium, and in this way, we can have an experience of previous productions. It is surprisingly easy to follow
the story of each play through these tableaus. By the time I
reach the auditorium, I feel as if I have been through an
abridged version of all the previous plays.

The hall widens at the end to allow multiple entrances
into the auditorium. Ushers scan us with the same devices as
before, which inputs into the devices our seat numbers. A
young man scans me, and he looks at his device. "G23," he
says, and his voice startles me because I have not heard anyone speak for maybe an hour now, and he guides me through
the door and to my seat.

#

The auditorium is full. No one speaks. I see the few people I recognize, such as Tom and Maddie, Mateo and Kate,
though they do not look at me. Now more than any time before there is the air of ceremony, the solemnity of religion,
and there is a pressure not to break the moment, and I do my
best to respect this moment some have waited for their entire
lives.

The last of the people sit down. The lights dim. And then there is an awful sound: the heavy doors shut and then something like metal locks slide into place. They lock us in.

A sensation brushes across the cloth of my jacket, and I look and there are metal locks over my wrists. I cannot move my hands. I look at the people next to me, expecting this to happen to everyone. But no one else is strapped in and everyone in the audience turns and looks at me.

I panic and I try to move my legs, but they are held in place, too, and there is a band around my torso. The curtain draws back, and the audience looks to the stage. And there on the stage is the body of Abby Edwards strapped to the chair that Takuya Usui built with the screen above it.

A woman walks across the stage. The audience claps. It takes me a moment to place the woman, but I do. She is Colleen, Abby's roommate. She stands before the microphone wearing the look of accomplishment, and the audience stands and applauds. Colleen raises her hand and waves at the audience, smiling.

"Thank you," she says, and the roar dies down. "Thank you," she says again. "It is my honor to welcome you to *Goat-Song V*. This year being our fifth anniversary—" and the crowd erupts into applause again. Colleen smiles and waits for the applause to subside. "This year being our fifth anniversary, we decided to reconnect ourselves to our roots. This year's theme reminded us of what we are."

A screen larger than the one attached to the chair in which Abby lies comes to life, and there I am on the screen speaking to Murasaki in her basement, our conversation captured on a hidden camera, and Murasaki's words echo throughout the auditorium: *"The goat is all that is earthly: violence, corruption, blood, fear, pain. The song is all that is eternal: peace, harmony, love, delight. In* Goat-Song, *the two are brought together as one."*

The screen goes black. Colleen clears her throat. The bands around my wrists and ankles tighten. "Let me introduce our team that has tirelessly worked to bring this year's *Goat-Song*—and maybe the most important *Goat-Song* we've ever had—to life."

A group of four people walk onto the stage. Two are Tom and Maddie. One is Kate. The fourth is the man I saw by the lake on the day my daughter drowned.

The small man by the lake walks to the microphone. He adjusts it down to his level. He takes a notecard from his pocket and reads from it. "Allow me to introduce the name of this year's *Goat-Song. Goat-Song V* from here and through the ages will forever be known as *Quantum Entanglement.*"

The crowd applauds. There are some in the audience who are so overwhelmed with emotion that they tear up. A hand is placed on my shoulder, but I cannot turn around to see who it is.

The small man steps away from the microphone and Tom walks to it. He readjusts the microphone to his height.

"I know this is the day we have all been waiting for," he says, "but we want to take a moment and recognize maybe the most important person on our team. Without her, none of this would have been possible. Please give it up for our Archeologist. And who better to be our archaeologist than the woman who can see through walls: Kate."

The crowd is bursting at the seams with excitement. Their applause is getting louder, almost manic, as the anticipation builds. The hand moves off my shoulder, and I feel vibrations from the back of my chair as someone is doing some kind of work on my seat.

Kate walks to the microphone. She smiles and the audience goes silent. "This is for you, Dad," she says. "Thanks to you, we can finish the work you started."

My chair tilts back. A strap is placed over my mouth. I struggle but it does nothing. I am carried, still strapped to the chair, down the aisle and toward the stage.

My voice is muffled as I yell for help, my legs are held in place as I kick, my arms are held in place as I grasp. I am raised onto the stage. Maddie walks to me. Colleen hands Maddie a needle that is filled with a black liquid. Maddie inserts the needle into my neck and discharges the liquid. The drug takes effect immediately. I cannot move, but I am still aware.

Stagehands roll out a giant glass container from backstage, twenty feet high and fifteen feet across. They set the container in place, return backstage and then roll out a second chair with a computer tower and a screen, identical to the one on which Abby lies. The metal clasps are loosened, the drug prevents me from moving, I am lifted from my chair and laid onto the other chair. A stagehand turns on the computer tower attached to the chair while others strap me in.

"As we wait for them to finish strapping Jamie in, let us look to some of this year's highlights."

They turn me so I can see the screen while they do their work. The screen is split in half. On the left side are projected scenes from my life, and on the right are scenes from Abby's life. As the two are shown side-by-side, they interweave and match and cross-over. There I am, dancing with Sarah, and there is Abby, dancing with her father. There I am, walking through the Usui's basement, wading through the hanging tapestries, and there is Abby, in another world, pushing aside similarly positioned tall weeds. There we are, making our way through the geode trees. There we are, mesmerized by chiming shapes. My own experiences are entangled with themselves, my dog is dead before it is hit, and I try but fail to save my Sarah twice. Abby and I have been living the same experiences, intertwined, she in another world, me here. We have been in a quantum entanglement.

I am the goat. She is the song. I am death. I am decay. I am humiliation. I am all that is transient and violent and unstable. She is royalty and honor and beauty and justice. And yet I am alive while she lies dead next to me.

The last images on the screen are of Abby coming into contact with the faceless entity with which I came into contact on the highway. She, as a kind of spirit, somehow wraps around it, and it becomes her. On my half of the screen, the creature stares at me in the car at night and then disappears as headlights shine into the car.

My half of the screen fades as Abby's fills the entire screen. There she is, strapped to the same chair, but in the other world. She wakes up there, and here, in front of me, Abby Edwards wakes from death. She is moving and speaking identically in both worlds.

"Hello?" she says. "What's going on?"

"Hello Abby," says Colleen.

"Who are you?" asks Abby.

"Abby," interjects Kate, "welcome." And Kate nods toward the others and then she turns and nods toward stagehands. Tom and Maddie walk to me, and the small man walks to Abby. "In just a moment," Kate continues, "you will be a part of history. You will help us, Abby. You will help us to bring to life that which we thought mere fantasy. You and Jamie are about to become the most important actors in the history of *Goat-Song*."

"Jamie?!" panics Abby and then an otherworldly creature wraps a strap over Abby's mouth on the screen just as Kate wraps a strap around Abby's mouth on stage.

Tom and Maddie take large cables that are attached to my chair's computer tower, and they hook it up to the large glass container. Tom walks to the small man and helps him do the same from Abby's computer tower to the same glass container.

A chill runs through me. Shostakovich's *Second Waltz* plays. The entire audience and some of the people on stage close their eyes in a kind of trance and hum along with it.

Kate walks to Abby's chair. She flips a switch on the computer tower. Abby's body goes rigid. On the screen, in the other world, Abby's body deflates, and in our world, her body goes lifeless. But in the glass container, maybe fifteen feet tall, slowly appears the faceless black entity, breathing and enormous. They removed it from inside Abby in the other world and brought it here.

Kate walks to my chair. I try to scream but nothing comes out. "Shh," says Kate, "we don't need your voice. Any creature can screech and howl. We need something from you that no other creature has. We need your human mind." I try to struggle but nothing happens. She flips the switch on my computer tower. My awareness goes electric, my mind's eye is blinded and for a moment there is nothing.

The sensation of nothingness passes instantaneously and over eons.

Then slowly I come to. There is pressure under my feet that was not present a moment ago. I am standing. I am inside the glass container. I look and see my lifeless body strapped to the chair. They transferred my awareness and my perception from my body into this creature.

And now, I am this massive creature standing in this glass container. I am slowly imbued with the memories of this creature, who more and more I realize is not another creature but now is me, and these are now my memories, and I remember who I am.

I once roamed this earth. I ruled in ages past. I have been caught between worlds, banished by the shaman millennia ago. But now I have returned.

I am all that is earthly and violent. I am all that is eternal and true. I am the goat and the song.

I step through the glass container as if it were immaterial. These are my subjects. I am their god. The music ends. All the people bow.

THE END

Gaps

1.

4cm.

The thing about gaps is that once you start noticing them you see them everywhere. Gaps between cars on the road, between buildings, between people talking. The more you consider them, the more complex they become. Some gaps are necessary, built into the fabric of reality, like the gaps between fruit trees so each can flourish. Some gaps are evil, like the gap between a withdrawn child and an abusive parent. Evil is perfectly designed to create gaps in relationships. Some gaps are imperceptible, like how my physicist friend told me that I am not really touching my table with my hands but there is an impenetrable and imperceptible gap between me and the table. There are even gaps in knowledge and understanding. Someone who studies a language closes the gap between their understanding and the language, but when they stop studying, the gap broadens. Gaps are real and immaterial, sometimes promoting good and flourishing and sometimes the result of evil and selfishness. And gaps are complex. The more I consider them, the more I realize there is more to know. Sometimes I wonder if maybe my life is itself one short gap inserted between the world before and after me. Or maybe I am real and wedged between two long

gaps of before me and after me. I am not sure which of those
is more terrifying.

One of the difficult things about gaps is that many times
they are unmanageable, though this does not always keep us
from trying to manage them. Sometimes, the gaps in relationships widen when we desperately try to pull them back
together, or maybe the gaps in relationships close when we
want them apart. Sometimes, the gap between today and tomorrow drags on no matter how frantically we want it
closed, or maybe it closes no matter how much we protest
for it to go on. Sometimes, sheer force does nothing to a gap,
as if the gap had purpose and honor and will, determined not
to be daunted by force or threat but splitting and splitting
until it finishes on its own terms. Those are the ones that
concern me.

Look at me, going on without context. I have been thinking about gaps because of what happened. One appeared in
my backyard. It was a small thing, probably no bigger than
an average sized fingernail or two. Four centimeters, if you
want to be more specific than fingernails. I did not know
where it came from or how it appeared. I have no children,
though I considered that maybe one of my neighbors' kids
did something. I also was not sure why I had the feeling that
it was caused intentionally. That I should be fixated on this
gap seems odd to me: Gaps and holes and crevices appear in
landscapes all the time as the result of earthquakes or perma-
frost or heavy rains. There are plenty of natural reasons for

gaps to occur in the ground. And yet I could not shake the feeling that this was intentional.

I first noticed the thing while sweeping my yard with my metal detector. The house I lived in was not officially historic, but it was historic enough, so metal detecting sometimes brought up odds and ends. My home was the town's hospital when settlers first arrived, so sometimes I found antique medical equipment. The town's settlers were mostly thieves and drunks. Makes you wonder why something as altruistic as building a hospital occurred to them, but they did it, nonetheless. I lived in the altruistic gap they built between their thieving and their drinking.

The day I found the gap, I was excited to do some metal detecting because I knew of valuable bottles buried in historic parts of town. Around that time, I had already found some old bottle caps in my backyard. The metal detector will not pick up the bottles, but if the bottles were anywhere near their old caps—or better yet, still had them on—I might be able to find them. So, I set out to where I found the bottlecaps the first time.

See, this is how I knew the gap was new and not something I had not noticed. My apologies: I do not mean to take it out on you. I get defensive about the situation with the gap. It was a hard thing to process, a strange gap opening up in your backyard. And I knew it was not there before because I carefully scoured the area after I found those first bottle caps.

I did not know what to make of it when I saw it. At first, I thought maybe the gap was a large black insect and I tried to shoo it away with my metal detector, but it did not move. Then I put the metal detector on the ground and took off the headphones and got on my knees to examine it.

The gap was a little black spot, like a kind of hole in the ground, and even though a hole is a perfectly good way to describe it, I thought of it as a gap. There was a faint hissing sound. I put my hand over the opening and felt air streaming out of it. The air fluttered in spurts, sometimes a steady stream and sometimes wavering about. I wondered if something was down there, moving the air about as it moved. Even though the opening was small, I suspected it was the same width all the way down. I could not see anything but blackness when I looked into it.

I think the reason the gap bothered me so quickly was because I did not leave my home much. I had no job to escape to or family to visit. Occasionally, friends visited me. My home was my world, so the gap was not a lawn-maintenance problem but an intruder. It was finding a spider in your bed right before you go to sleep.

By the way, I don't know if you know this: *Shoo* is short for *bashoo*, and *bashoo!* is the sound that elephants make right before they trample otherwise healthy Europeans when they get too close. In parts of South Africa, as unsuspecting Europeans close in, the elephant raises its trunk, and before the European knows the score, the elephant says *bashoo! bashoo!* and that's the end of that.

2.

10cm.

A night or two after I discovered the gap, I had a nightmare. The dream was one of those falling dreams that inflates your stomach, but the falling did not wake me. I fell and fell into the gap as it widened and widened. But the terror was not found in the falling. The terror was the blackness of the gap. As I fell, the blackness was living, and it took me in. As I fell, the little bit of light I could see out of the corner of my eyes faded. And then I stopped falling. I became a part of that blackness. I knew it, and it knew me, knower and known in living relationship, and I knew myself as I was because I knew it—and I could not escape knowing and being known by it. The terror was not in dying but in being alive in and being known by the blackness as I became a part of it. In the midst of my terror, I realized that no one would find me as the blackness knew me deeper and deeper.

Then I awoke.

I got out of bed and looked out of my window and into my backyard and saw that the gap widened. It at least doubled in size. There was clearly a gap in my yard, no mistaking it for a bug. The blades of grass around the gap flickered from the air streaming out of it.

Then I turned from the window to my bed. And there was the egg.

Scout's honor is what I offer you: There was a real life unbroken healthy egg. Not a small one, either, like a salmon egg or a chicken egg, but more like the size, shape and consistency of an ostrich egg.

Funny how much pride a person can have who lives alone and who does not have much contact with other people. You might think not being around others makes it easier to be yourself without being self-conscious or proud, but this is not the case. For example, sometimes I would not watch movies I secretly wanted to watch in case it somehow came out that I watched it or even liked it. Pride is a funny thing. It opens false gaps in our lives, pretending there are gaps where there are none. The reason I say this is because, looking back, the truth is that my pride made it hard for me to consider the terrifying fact that I may have laid the egg.

I say "may have" because I am not sure. I have never laid an egg before then or since, so I do not know what laying one feels like. I know that I did not feel like I laid one. Nothing about my body felt different. But there the egg was nonetheless, so it must have come from somewhere. And it was in my bed, in the spot I slept. And here my pride tempts me to hold back, but I will say it anyway. As soon as I saw the egg, I was less shocked by its existence and more shocked by my protective instincts welling up inside me. I suddenly cared deeply for the well-being of this egg. For a moment, I even forgot about the gap in the backyard. All I considered was how to keep the egg healthy.

It was strange to suddenly care so much for something I had not seen before. I did not care an ounce for some of my neighbors, many of whom I had known for years. But the egg had a grip on me, and I could not tell if it was the kind of grip that comes with love or the kind of grip that comes with obsession. Either way, the grip transcended me, and I was caught in it.

Both love and obsession transcend the individual. Makes you wonder if there is such a thing as a transcendent gap.

3.

10cm.

I went to the store to get the supplies to build a bed for the egg. Usually, I put off going to the store for as long as I could, stocking up on dried, canned and frozen goods, determined to stay in my home. What was strange was that going to the store was not a chore. I wanted to get supplies for the egg. There was something about the egg that was bigger than me, and I could not have been happier to get into my car and drive to the store, like a young boy happy to have a new responsibility.

During the trip to the store, though, the people around town would not or maybe could not stop staring at me. There were a lot of shifty eyes. This was not my imagination either. I watched two people on the sidewalk bump into each other because they were both staring at me.

Let me be clear: It was not odd that people stared at me. Well, it was, and it wasn't. What was odd was that people remembered to stare at me. It had been so long since they did. You see, I used to be well known around town. This was before I holed up in my house. I was a kind of scholar, and by that, I mean, I had an education but was not employed anywhere scholarly. The town designated me its honorary professor. I knew a bit about things like the town's history and nearby animal and plant life. Sometimes, the local paper asked me my opinion about environmental or political issues, or the mayor took photos with me if I happened to be around during something mayoral. But one day I awoke, and I could no longer go along with this charade any longer. Some people called it a nervous breakdown. But I was under no pressure of any kind. And I enjoyed what I did. What happened was that I woke up at my limit.

At the end of the book of Job, God confronts Job and tells him that God is able to set limits and boundaries to individual realities within the whole of reality. God designed the waves to end at the shores and come no further. God made the ostrich without wisdom, with a gap in her knowledge, that her eggs warming in the sand may be trampled underfoot. And no matter how hard the ostrich or the waves try, they cannot break through to the other side of the limits of their reality. But God makes it clear that a larger reality can break through to them.

This is not that different from what happened to me. I woke up one day at the limits of my reality. Like I said, some thought I had a nervous breakdown or maybe I went insane. And maybe there was some truth in it. For a while, people around town stared at me, whispering to each other when I passed by. That was when I started staying home.

During my trip to the store, enough time passed that most people did not know about my isolation, barely remembered it or were comfortable enough with it to be polite. This was why it was odd that people stared at me. They had not stared at me for a long time and nothing that I knew of changed, so I could not imagine why they should start again.

Funny how a certain amount of comfort with a situation is required to be polite. It is hard to be polite in the face of something you have never experienced or imagined. Maybe those who daydream about the end of the world will be the most polite when it comes.

So, what was my mind frame when I drove to the store? This is a fair question. I will answer it since you and I are kind of like survivors stuck with each other on a raft adrift at sea. It is only fair you know enough about me to judge my

words for yourself. At the time my frame of mind was somewhere around *I don't care anymore* and *I couldn't do something about it even if I wanted to.*

4.

10cm.

After I returned from the store, I made a bed for the egg.
Let me rephrase that. It is probably more accurate to call the
bed a nest, though at the time I could not handle calling it
that. The bed certainly resembled a nest. I put the nest in my
bedroom and made it out of a circular wooden frame stuffed
with towels and lamps around it to keep the egg warm. It
took me some time, and I was proud of the work I did. Pride
was a feeling I had not felt in a while.

After I made the bed and plugged in all of the lamps, I
put the egg into its bed. And then I heard a noise. But it was
not an additional noise. It was the kind of sound you hear
when a sound you have heard for days—a kind of sound you
no longer hear because it is a constant sound—suddenly
stops. I looked outside at the gap and saw that the grass
leaves were no longer flickering. Air no longer streamed out
of the gap. I realized that up until that time I heard the hissing of the air.

And then I heard another noise. It was the sound of the egg falling against something hard. The egg was no longer in its bed, but it rolled and was wedged in a gap between the bed and bed frame.

5.

60cm.

Under the pretense of gardening, I spent a part of the afternoon studying the gap. The gap was now wide enough to be able to throw things into it. I was correct to suspect the gap to be deep. I shined a flashlight down its mouth but could not see the bottom. I threw a stone into it and only heard the stone bounce off the earthen sides for a split second and heard nothing more. I did not hear the rock hit the bottom, assuming there was one. I walked to a shaded part of the yard and drank some water. Then I heard the latching sound of my backyard gate.

It was my neighbors' son. The child was young, maybe six or seven, the kind of age where inviting yourself over is not rude. I could not remember his name, so I said, "What are you doing here?" He paused for a moment and then smiled, thinking my bluntness was a joke.

"I'm coming to see what you're doing," he said.

"Gardening."

"Can I help?" he asked.

"No."

"What's that?" he asked, pointing to the gap, and before I could answer, he was on his hands and knees peering straight into it.

"Don't—"

But he did.

I ran to the gap and looked in. There was no trace of him. I half expected the gap to belch.

By that evening, I still had not said anything to anyone. I could hear a search party calling the boy's name, but I did nothing. I went to bed contemplating how to break the news to my neighbors in the morning. Little did I realize I would not have the opportunity.

You know, most people think birds cannot belch but this is not true. There is a rare type of bird that lives in parts of New Zealand that not only can belch but can drink through a straw. In ancient times, the bird was revered as a god until they discovered that its ability to belch made its meat tender and less odorous than that of other birds. Its scientific name is *Zealandia gastricus* but more commonly it is referred to as a beezle.

6.

1.5m.

During the night, after the neighbors' child fell into the gap, there was a rumbling, and I knew the gap widened. After the rumbling ceased, I glanced at the egg to make sure it was still in its bed. I saw the egg wobbling. The low setting of the dim red heat lamp did not give off much light but enough for me to be certain of what I saw. I got out of bed and walked to the egg, and it was still wobbling. And its wobbling increased, spasming, shaking, the sight disturbing and exhilarating, and I could not understand it and yet my instincts to care for the egg knew that this was normal and good. And then it stopped.

I went back to my bed and got under my covers. I made sure my feet were under the covers. I do not know why I feel unsafe when my feet are uncovered while I try to sleep, as if an overly vulnerable part of me is exposed.

And then there was a light. Not a small light or a light from inside my house. It was a light from the outside, like massive searchlights were turned on and pointed at my bedroom window, drenching everything in a stunning whitish blue outpour. The lights had a direction, and its direction was me—directed at my house and through my windows, so bright it drowned the light from the heat lamp, intending only to reach me. It did not come from my neighbors. It did not come from this world.

Cracks formed in my windows, and the light splintered through the cracks, playing off the dust and the light. The light streaming through the cracks formed shadowy lines in the air and on the bedroom wall. I turned to the wall and saw that there was design to them, like an ancient script or hieroglyphics, animating and being written as the cracks in the windows spread with purpose. Something was communicating with me. My house was a zoetrope with the light shining in from the outside and the cracks in the windows forming shadowy figures.

On the wall was a kind of animation. Maybe a story is a better way to put it. On the wall was what looked like a tiny spot. And the spot was the gap, and it grew until out popped an egg. Clearly not just any egg but the egg. And the egg jumped into the arms of a person-type figure. But the gap continued to grow, and it swallowed people, houses, buildings, trees, animals. The larger the gap became, the more it became clear that it did not grow at a steady pace, but there was a kind of pulsing, sometimes shrinking just a bit before growing again. The gap was breathing, inhaling and exhaling.

Then there appeared what looked like an animal of some sort. A ragged looking reptilian creature, nothing immediately recognizable. There was a simple crudeness to its representation and the crudeness made it all the more horrifying. The image of the creature first appeared to the side of the wall as the gap grew. But it crept closer to the egg and to the figure holding the egg. The creature stopped. Then the gap made its way toward the figure and the egg. Then the gap and the creature moved together, and the two worked to corner the figure and the egg. The gap and the creature trapped the figure and the egg, and the creature was about to overtake them—

But I did not see the rest. Because at that moment, I heard a low and otherworldly reptilian growl just outside my bedroom door. The cracking windows shattered to dust, and I grabbed the egg and I jumped out of the window and I ran.

7.

1.5m.

You may think that I ran to the police or to someone with the authority and knowledge to use a weapon in public. Here you are forcing me to admit that I have been keeping a secret from you.

My apologies: I acknowledge that it is unfair of me to blame you, saying things like *you are forcing me*. Like I said before, I get defensive when it comes to explaining the situation with the gap. Forgive me for keeping this from you and not telling you at the start. This is no way to treat one's life-raft partner.

The truth, as you may have already suspected, is more complicated than saying I came to the limits of my reality. You probably suspected something when I did not immediately tell my neighbors that their son fell into the gap, which is what any sane or moderately compassionate person would have done. The truth is that I committed a kind of fraud and was publicly exposed for it. Since then, there has been an unspoken agreement between me and the town: I have permission to stay but only under the strict conditions that I leave my house as little as possible and interact with no town-related workers, such as public officials, first responders and real estate agents. You may have heard of a DNR: do not resuscitate. I have something similar. I have a DNAIAWW: do not assist in any way whatever.

Funny how it is possible to measure the distance societies evolve by the increase in length of their legal customs and language. For example, consider a real estate transaction today with a real estate transaction in ancient Israel. In ancient Israel, real estate was exchanged with a simple yes or no in front of the elders and the removing of a sandal. Today, the exchange of real estate is something similar to a coming-of-age bureaucratic sport where every move is a personal foul, and all the players are referees.

This concept of the evolution of legalese in a society as the measure of the complexity of its customs holds true in my case. My DNAIAWW is today's legalese equivalent of Hester Prynne's A.

8.

50m.

What happens when beings outside your world communicate with you? How do you respond? How do you judge what is true? What if you received multiple communications that seemed to contradict each other? How would you determine what is true from what is false? I understand now why in alien movies the writers who get into the heads of their characters portray the people who encounter aliens for the first time as hesitating. You do not know if the aliens are friendly or not. The situation is unprecedented. You do not know how they think, if they have morals, what they want, that is, assuming they have the capacity to want. You cannot make a move until they make one first that you understand. And that last part is crucial. It is not just any move that must be made, but an intelligible one.

After jumping out of the window and running across my backyard, I went into the foothills behind the town, not far from my house. The time between jumping out of the window and running to the foothills was already a blur by the time I got to the foothills. That moment between the growl of the beast and my finding myself in the foothills lapsed so quickly and so instinctually that I hardly had time to catch myself. I considered that maybe it was one of those hallucinations you have right when you wake up, the kind where you hear someone speaking or you see a spider descending next to you. The weirdness with the egg made the situation somewhat more plausible, but I was not convinced that something real happened.

I looked down the foothill and saw my house and yard, and just as I began seriously contemplating returning to my house, I saw the gap increase in size. My house was in a well-lit neighborhood for nighttime, plus my jumping out of the window triggered the floodlights' sensors, so my backyard was clearly visible even from this distance. That was the first time I saw the gap grow as it happened. Until that moment, I came across the gap only after it grew. When the gap grew, it certainly had the look of breathing.

If you asked me to describe what it was like to watch the gap grow, I would describe the situation by saying that it was not unpleasant to watch but I would not want to watch it again. Somewhere between a field of roses and livestock giving birth. If that helps.

The rim of the gap resembled jagged edges alongside steep ocean cliffs. The edges gave way, the cliffs crumbled, the ground shook and the gap grew. The gap forged through the ground in the direction of my house. And then my house fell into the gap. This was a tremendous blow to my entire life, and it happened silently in the night in seconds while my neighbors dreamed of microwave dinners and television commercials.

In the orange glow of the streetlamps, I saw the creature creep down the street, away from the foothills. The creature either had lost track of me and the egg, or it was not interested at the moment.

I know now why these kinds of moments are described as having gravity, like when someone says *the gravity of the moment*. This is because these moments anchor you back to a reality from which everyday monotony slowly lifts you without you realizing it. Moments with gravity undo the gradual eroding and disillusionment of everyday *stuff*, stuff which slowly disconnects you from the plane of reality like an astronaut adrift in space.

9.

50m.

In my study of the town's history, I learned that nearly one hundred years ago the town had immigrant shepherds who journeyed along the foothills and built small shelters under which they slept. There was a chain of them across the foothills as the shepherds lead their sheep through the grass and drank from the mountain runoff that ran through the ravines. I did not know the location of all of the shelters, but I knew that one of them was near my house, so I made my way to it.

To call it a shelter may be misleading for some, so I will be clear. It was a hammock hanging from a roof. There was a single pole supporting the roof and to which one side of the hammock was tied. This was enough to keep the shepherds off the ground and dry, but without walls so the shepherds could keep an eye on their sheep during the night. The hammock was slightly upright, presumably so the shepherds could quickly get out of bed if urgent needs arose, with the head of the hammock tied to the roof and the feet of the hammock tied to the base of the pole.

I laid on my back in the hammock with the egg on my stomach rolled in my shirt. The hammock was sturdy and somewhat newer and therefore probably not an original left-over from the shepherds but used by modern transients. I considered my situation with the egg. At first, I thought that maybe the reptile creature was the mother of the egg, and maybe the creature was being protective. But this seemed unlikely. If the story on the wall were true, it seemed much more to be the case that the egg was escaping from the reptile creature.

That is as far as I contemplated before hitting a wall. I did not know what else to do or where else to go. My survival instincts suggested I try to sleep to have the energy to do something the next day, so that is what I did. Throughout the night, the periods of sleep and the periods of wakefulness changed imperceptibly and mostly it seemed like I stayed awake the whole night.

Here is an interesting aside: In Portugal, there were sand shepherds whose work consisted in guiding sand dunes as they traveled inland from the coast. These sand shepherds were called *aldosuevas*, roughly translated as "hump gatherers." Unfortunately, *aldosuevas* no longer refers to this noble work, but to those who gather and sell plastic bowls.

10.

50m.

I did not dream that night. The sky was gray and the sun nearly risen. I stood out of the hammock. I unraveled my shirt and felt the egg. It was cold. There was no motion, and I realized there was no motion from the egg all night.

I panicked. I breathed on it, trying desperately to warm it. But nothing happened. I wept.

The egg trusted me, and I failed it. It looked to me for protection, and I ran from the creature instead of fighting it. My cowardice and the half-truths that came out of the gap between me and myself affected something else in a way that I finally saw and understood.

I held the egg to my cheek in undaunted hopefulness, and as I did, I felt a small motion from inside. The egg was not dead. But it was not well. I knew what I had to do.

My legs shook and my eyesight blurred as I walked back to my house, fighting my terror. I was tired from lack of sleep, but there was a sharp manic clarity about me, an anger and determination to do what I needed to do. A woman scorned may bring something greater than hell's fury, but a man shamed brings something greater than heaven's wrath.

The hillside morphed as I walked down it. I sunk and rose like a boat at sea. Not only the ground moved me, but everything seemed to move me. The sunrise broke and shed colorful light on the foothills and the valley, and in those colors I saw that it was not only the ground that rose and fell but all the world around me: the misty air, the houses, the trees, the mountains, the sky. The gap inhaled and exhaled, and its inhaling and exhaling disrupted not only the ground but reality itself. All of reality vibrated with waves and billows emanating from the gap inhaling and exhaling.

There was no one around. I did not know if the people fled or vanished or fell into the gap. There was a silence over the town, and I seemed to be the last one left.

I arrived at my backyard and heard a low growl. I looked and saw the creature. It was reptilian and had the gait of a Komodo dragon and about double the size. It had horns on its head, a long tail, webbed claws and dull scales hinting blue and green.

I approached the gap and the creature approached me. I looked into the gap. To my surprise, there was more than blackness inside it. There was a distant but clear light. The light was moving, living, rotating. It spread in fractals, changing colors and shapes. It was wonderous and beautiful.

And then the egg hatched.

I would tell you what it was that came out of the egg, but the truth is that I did not look at it. It was not that I did not want to or was too scared to look. It was that I knew all I needed to know about the egg. It was precious. And that was enough.

The beast came closer at a quicker pace, its growl heightening to a terrifying screech. The beast lunged, but it did not touch me, for I closed my eyes, held the egg close to my chest, and I let us fall into the gap.

END

Poison

1

Up To Speed
(July 2032)

Let me get you up to speed. In October of 2031 the U.N. established sanctions on my small business. There's a wall around it now with barbed wire and a security checkpoint at the only entrance. Business was going fine before. It was the best it has ever been. I kept a full-time staff with full benefits. An employee once gave me a gift. It was a bottle opener in the shape of a shark. I still have it. I don't drink alcohol.

I am in the food industry, but I am not allowed to tell you what I sell. It can fit comfortably in a grown-man's hand, if that helps. Most people eat a version of it. I cannot tell you directly what it is because that might violate a sanction, since I am not allowed to trade with most of what we call the Civilized World. *To civilize* is a verb which means to bring out of savagery or barbarism. Civility is not a measure of internal harmony but of external utility. When I was younger, I used to hold the door open for people. Now, I sell something the U.N. tells me not to sell. When I was younger, I was civilized. Now I am not.

The best part of having U.N. sanctions against you is that you become an instant celebrity in North Korea and Cuba. Iran does not care one way or the other. My enemies are now

151

my friends, and my friends are now my enemies. I used to hold the door open for people and now they shut doors in my face. It's a funny world. Civilized, but funny.

October is when the sanctions began, but what led to them started in August. That was when I discovered the secret ingredient that made my palm-sized snack so tasty. There is a curiosity as to how up-in-arms people got over my secret ingredient, one that I cannot explain very well. My secret ingredient may be poisonous, as was later claimed, but in the short time that I sold it, the customers did not seem to notice. On the contrary, my customer repeat was the envy of the likes of chain restaurants and big tech. During my short tenure, not one person became sick or died eating my product. Due to poison, I mean. And without synthesizing the poison by itself. I cannot control people who choke. I bet some people died without me knowing because they choked. But they could hardly be considered repeat customers.

The U.N. does not put sanctions on pretzel makers. Pretzels are made with a lye glaze. Lye is a poison that is used in drain cleaners. I guess it is the kind of poison, when it comes down to it. Lye has a precedent while mine does not. No one has seen such a thing before I made it. Lye kicked down doors to a new era and shut doors behind it. My poison is more civilized. It holds the door open for poisons coming in after it. I think that might be the problem the U.N. has with my product. The trouble is not necessarily the poison itself but that for which it opens the door.

Although the product has been labeled broadly as poison, I do not use it as one, unlike others. I use my product for a tasty snack. People in more savage parts of the world use it as a weapon or a drug. If uncivilized people used my food for food to keep their bodies in motion to do bad things to civilized people, then no one would bat an eye at me any more than someone might bat an eye at corn growers. But uncivilized people do not use my secret ingredient merely as sustenance. Instead, uncivilized people use my food for weapons to do bad things to civilized people.

North Korea and Cuba like my product. They even like it for food. Their citizens know what is in it, too. My secret ingredient is not a secret over there. It does not bother them because it tastes so good, just like people here like pretzels.

But what is poison, anyway? How do we decide what is considered poisonous and what is not? If I were to drink nothing but olive oil, I would die, yet olive oil is not a poison. Some insect bites will take days to kill a person. Some hamburgers will take years to do the same. But it is the eventual ease that confuses me. Both insect bites and hamburgers accomplish the same job just as easily, given enough time.

This may be part of the problem. For the Civilized World, that is. There is an anxiety as to how easily poison will take a life, almost like a magic trick. It is the uncertainty that makes us squirm in our chairs. Man puts hand in hat. In unseen places, man grabs rabbit. Man pulls rabbit out. This is magic.

Poison is not that different. Man drinks poison. In unseen places, poison dissolves life. Man crumples and dies. Ta-da.

I think magic tricks bother civilized people more than uncivilized. Partly because of our lack of faith in unseen things. Now that we are civilized, we have been brought out of barbarism, and this is a status we feel obligated to maintain and especially to announce to the world that we maintain. Faith is for barbaric people. Civilized people do not need faith. We need facts and numbers. False certainty is better than blind faith. Is it not?

Poison can stop lungs from functioning and taking in oxygen. But why does breathing keep life going? Why does the brain need oxygen? Why will oxygen allow one to watch *I Love Lucy* one minute and then crumple and die the next? Even at its most micro level, modern science is still only the appearance of things. Civilized people rely too much on the appearance of things. The magic is gone from our lives. It was eaten away by poison. And by *I Love Lucy*. *I Love Lucy* had a precedent.

Writing can be a kind of poison, too. Writing can create ideas and take them away just like magic tricks. Moses wrote God made the world in six days. God created Man in His own image. Science wrote Man evolved from Ape's own image. Magic crumpled and died.

Ta-da.

2

A Sort of Nutty Flavor
(August 2031)

I met Colonel Vernon Ooberdoober in September, not long after I discovered my poison. I particularly remember his bolo tie. He was not naked, but he could have been naked, and I might not have noticed under less intense circumstances. Most people who wear bolo ties could be totally nude, and I normally would not notice. Not many things are more distracting than nudity. The person who invented the bolo tie should be proud.

For the sake of clarity, I have to say that I met Colonel Vernon in September and that I discovered my poison in August. The truth is that both things happened mere minutes apart. On August 31st, close to midnight, I was in my garage fermenting gases and yeasts. My palm-sized snack needed something that tastes like a considerable amount of time has passed through it. Sort of like putting food in the microwave, only waiting longer. I irradiated my food with time.

The condensed time gathered in a vial, and I drank it. Not many people know this, but time has a sort of nutty flavor. If you were to open your mouth and stay in one place for a few hours, you would understand.

I drank the creation and waited for a few minutes to see

how the flavor played. Some people call the taste after ingestion "the aftertaste." To me, this is nothing more than time added to the flavor. This may be comparable to eating a salty chip and pouring more salt in your mouth. The flavor was good. There was not so much an aftertaste as an after-effect. You see, in high and concentrated doses, it is not only the flavor that plays, but it is memory. And it is not always your memory.

I felt faint and dizzy. A cross-breeze of memories flooded my mind. These memories were the memories of someone who fought in World War II. Someone who fought from the air. There were images of countrysides and coasts, all seen from high vantage points. There was the inside of a cockpit and shouting. There were buttons and switches, levers and bullets. There was a shot and the world spun and screamed. The world spun and spun and spun and I got closer and closer to the ground and just as the images in my mind were about to crash, I heard something crash outside of my garage.

Time has a nutty flavor to it: Fermented and nutty. I looked at my watch. It was 12:01AM. It was September.

3

A Blue Camry
(September 2031)

I opened my garage and there was a helicopter on my front lawn. The helicopter was not very impressive looking, when compared with modern ones. It was covered in bullet-holes. The pilot came out. He was not hurt but he was highly agitated.

He threw his helmet to the ground and pulled out his pistol. He pointed it at the windows, the neighbor's cat, the horizon. He was not sure where to point it, I figured, so he covered all his bases.

"Where am I?" he asked. "What happened?"

The street lights went out. It was dark. The lights lit again.

"What kind of car is that?" He pointed the pistol at my car.

"A Camry," I said. "It's blue."

"What's a Camry?"

"It's a Toyota. It's Japanese."

He pointed the pistol at me. "Sweet Eleanor Roosevelt, have you lost your mind? Why would you buy a Japanese car?" He walked to me with his pistol unwavering.

"It's reliable and the gas mileage—"

"Do you know who I am?"

"No."

"I am Colonel Vernon Ooberdoober, and if you don't tell me what's going on, I'm going to shoot you where you stand."

I looked at my feet to see if I stood in a dignified place to die. I stood in cat poop. I stepped to the left.

"I'm going to count to three and if—"

And Colonel Vernon Ooberdoober disappeared along with the helicopter. The memory of the Colonel was gently blown from my reality. "That was weird," I said to myself.

I sat on the grass, grabbed a small stick, and I cleaned the poop off my shoe. Stick-cleaning took me twenty minutes. I gagged twice.

4

A Month's Span
(July 2032)

I met the memory of Colonel Vernon Ooberdoober in September. The U.N. placed sanctions on me in October.

September.

October.

The above is a month's span. You can hold up your thumb and index finger to measure the distance between the two. As you can see, this is, at most, only about an inch. If anyone asks you how long a month is, now you can show them with confidence. A month is not very long.

5

Which of the Impacts
(September 2031)

The next day I stole my neighbor's cat. I wanted to feed it my poison, my secret ingredient, to see how it responded. I did not realize until after I experimented on myself that this method was a much more efficient way to go about experimenting. I should have done it first. Cat obits do not wind up in a newspaper when bits o' cat wind up on a street. As my mother used to say.

Getting the cat was not as hard as I expected. I opened my front door, and the cat was on my welcome mat. I bent down, I picked it up, I shut the door. Easy as that.

I decided the best way to make the cat drink the liquid was to make it thirsty. Resourceful as I am, I found an old hair dryer, held the cat's mouth open, and blasted it with hot air for a few seconds. Then I poured the secret ingredient into a water dish. The cat drank the water.

The lights in my house flickered and buzzed. The cat closed its eyes and bent back its ears. A memory came across the cat's mind. A memory from somewhere else, floating in the air across time. The cat was an antenna and it picked up the memory.

The cat convulsed, and it leapt across the room as though it leapt out of the way of a moving vehicle. Please excuse me. I should not say *as though*, because the truth is that that is exactly what the cat did. The cat leapt out of the way just in time not to be hit by a moving car that appeared in my living room and rammed into my kitchen wall. The driver put her hands over her face out of instinct before she hit the wall. The airbag did not deploy. The driver died from the impact. The driver was my wife who died in a car accident three years earlier. She was alive when she first appeared in my living room. I saw her put her hands up.

I do not know what happens when someone dies in a memory. If they are alive when the memory manifests, that is. Even now, I am not quite sure. Today, with as rampant as everything became, we have all seen someone die in memories, since the sanctions have been placed. There is an uncertainty that envelops us now and currently no one knows the answer. When someone dies in a memory brought to life, that person is already dead in present reality. What we do not know is if the memory killed them and thus changed our memory of them from being alive to being dead, or if they were truly dead to begin with.

In other words, there is something I do not know: If I had not made my poison, would my wife still be alive? Did she die in a car accident three years earlier in order to balance out, so to speak, her death in my kitchen three years later?

And which of the impacts was the one that killed her? Was it the building she ran into downtown or the wall in my kitchen? Could it be both?

The manifested memory flickered and flashed away. My wall was destroyed. The cat ran out of the hole in the kitchen wall.

6

Impacts
(July 2032)

It took me a while to realize, but now we all know. People who drink my product in its purest form pick up on memories related to what the imbiber put into his or her mind. I watched a lot of World War II movies and documentaries, so I picked up on that kind of memory. The cat picked up on someone who had the memory of watching my wife die.

Now that it is illegal to buy and trade my product, some drug dealers traffic it from North Korea. There are factories dedicated to extracting the secret ingredient. North Korea has huge quantities of it, thanks to Russia. The drug dealers then traffic the extraction to America, and they sell it to murderers and psychopaths and pornographers. It is sold to a great variety of voyeurs.

There are fatalities because of all the illegal trafficking.

Murderers who drink my poison are then visited by the memory of other murderers who kill the user. Porn addicts ingest in the hope of having wild orgies. Instead, they are raped and given diseases by their manifested memories. Some diseases have made a resurgence, because people in these memories bring the diseases to the present. The number of smallpox cases is slowly growing. The number of syphilis cases is growing faster. Most doctors who study medicine will not take my secret ingredient out of respect for humanity.

There are some people who try to win a kind of lottery. For example, there are some who intensely study history in the hopes of manifesting a memory of some great historical figure. Those who strive for these manifestations record themselves and the memories they experience and post the recordings online. One man in the Democratic Republic of the Congo recorded himself speaking with what most scholars agree was probably a confused Plato. The Congolese man studied Ancient Greek philosophy and language day in and day out in order to bring about such a memory. He was awarded an honorary degree from Pyongyang University.

Memory Rights advocates, as they have come to be called, decry such behavior. These advocates argue for the rights memories have to stay in the past and not to be exposed to the present. They want to ban posting online videos, especially the more vulgar ones, such as those of pranks pulled on the manifested memories. Just this morning I watched a video of a group of college kids who sprayed the memory of a family with a hose.

I do not pay much attention to what is going on. I have my own memories to tend to. I do not need those of anyone else anymore.

7

Risk Taking More
(September 2031)

It took me three days to get over the shock of seeing my dead wife. Once I did, I went to the United States Patent and Trademark Office. I figured it would be difficult to get a patent for a poison. At this time, I first called it my secret ingredient. Little did I know, all kinds of poisons have patents, even the atom bomb has one, so asking for a patent for a poison was no biggie.

There was not much of a line or a wait. I guess not many people invent new things these days. The lady at the counter was very old. The older a person gets, the more difficult it is to pinpoint exactly what my secret ingredient will do and what kind of memory will manifest. With as many days behind her as this lady had, it is a wonder what kind of memories she would pick up. With as many days behind her as this lady had, it is a wonder she could drag them so easily in her invisible burlap sack. The thing must have weighed a ton. A month might not be very long, but a day is heavier than you think.

"Can I help you?" she asked.

"I'd like to patent this, please," I said. I slid my formula to her like movie characters negotiating large amounts of money. It was face-down, too, and on the top, I stenciled the words "secret ingredient."

She flipped it over. She read it. "OK," she said. She held out documents for me to fill.

"When can I expect my patent?"

"This takes time."

"Can you risk taking more?"

"What?"

I took the papers, sat down, and filled out the papers. Bureaucracy is not kind to the elderly. Bureaucracy makes them wait for something that might not happen. On the other hand, Fascism is not kind to the young. Fascism takes away time from those who do not yet have it.

You cannot win them all.

8

Dreams and Goals
(November 2031)

Unsurprisingly, I became popular with dictators after the sanctions were placed. The North Korean dictator called me. I do not remember which Kim he was, but he was a Kim, nonetheless.

One day my phone rang. I answered and a recording said, *"Hello, will you accept a collect call from…"*

A man came on. With great honor and emphasis, he said in his nasal voice, "His Humble and Majestic Great Leader of the Free Communist World, Kim—" The recording cut-off.

"By accepting the call, you also accept the long-distance charges. Do you accept?"

How could I not? There were two firsts for me in one go. Until then, I had not talked to a Communist leader. I had spoken to the president, but that is different. Until then, I also had not received a collect call. I did not know people still did such a thing.

"Hello?" I asked. I do not know why I ask hello every time I answer the phone. Hello is a greeting, not a question. If I were honest and had no social conscience, I would simply pick up a phone and ask *Who is this?*

"Hello," said the nasal voice. "My name is Hyo, I am

translator for His Humble and Majestic Great Leader of the—"

"Hello, Hyo."

"Hello."

" … "

" … "

"What can I do for you?"

"His Humble and Majest—"

"What can I do for you and Kim?" I asked.

"We like your product. We like it very much. We want to trade," he said.

"I can't trade," I said. "There are sanctions on my business."

There were whispers. Hyo spoke. "We understand. North Korea is not part of U.N. We can help you do secret trade. We like your product very much."

"How can we trade in secret?" I looked outside. "I'm looking out my window now. There are men building concrete walls and putting barbed wire around my store. I can't get anything in or out."

"You go to Alaska," said Hyo, "and we will do the rest. I will send you a map."

"Alaska?"

The line disconnected.

I looked out of my window. The U.N. contractors building the wall and fence were chatting with each other as though they were building a dog house for a friend. They laughed and joked. One man pointed to a hammer and another politely grabbed it for him. People pick strange times to be polite.

It was not their livelihoods they were caging. The barbed wire was not meant for them. What did they care? They had their own dreams and goals to accomplish.

But Alaska? Why the Kim would I want to go back to Alaska?

9

Degrees and Dollars
(July 2032)

I would say I had no other choice, but that is a lie. I did not have to deal with any dictator. I could have stopped selling my product altogether. When the country you live in puts up barbed wire around your business, and the country you are against lends a helping hand, it is easy to rationalize friendships. If your best friend were to push you down and the bully at school were to help you up, the bully would not seem so bad.

Besides, in small doses, my poison is not poisonous. It is quite delicious. There are no strange memory effects. I did not want to make a poison, but I wanted to live the American Dream, whether America would let me or not: I wanted to make the most amount of money in the quickest amount of time doing the least amount of work. Why else would I have a college degree?

College seems so silly now. I believed I could pay money to make myself more valuable. I was naive. Measuring human value with college degrees and dollars.

Now, I sell my product in many countries. It is beyond my control if they do more with my product than eat it. People make shovels even though shovels are used to bury murder victims. I sell the product. I do not sell the intention. People do not need my intentions. They have enough as it is.

10

Selfish People
(November 2031)

Not long after I talked to Hyo, I got a text message from Fidel Castro. I'm not sure how he got my number. It does not surprise me that he found my number. I think cigar smokers have a mysteriousness about them that non-smokers will never understand. If he told me he could fly with his mind, I would believe him.

I texted directly to Castro without a translator. Castro warned me about doing business with certain countries. He said North Korea was not a big deal. He said to be careful of other Asian countries. Some African ones, too. *There aren't people who seek evil* his text warned. *There are selfish people who seek.*

I did not listen to his warning.

Now I see I was not evil. I wanted to live the American Dream. I was a selfish person who sought. I valued myself in dollars and degrees.

11

Crazy is Easy to Hide
(September 2031)

I discovered investors are a lot like children. In three ways, actually. First, investors do not understand much without pictures and diagrams. Second, investors think bows and stickers improve the quality of a product. Third, investors want the false comfort of knowing you know more about the future than they do.

While I waited for my patent, I baked my palm-sized product at home. By diluting the poison and then baking it, I found the memory effect all but vanished. The product still left a hint of the taste and a mild psychological jogging. There was enough to pique an interest but not enough for the consumer to know what happened.

I visited local food joints, bars and such, to see if they would sell it. I assumed that because I am Me and Me made it, they would want it. Most people turned it down. I think they thought I was a crazy person trying to poison them. In a way, they were right. It did not help that I brought the food on paper plates and plastic wrap.

So, I sold some of my wife's old clothing and belongings for extra cash. Seeing her did not make me want to hold onto those things anymore. I used the cash to design fancier packaging and labels and stickers.

When I brought the potential business partners my product with the new look, they did not think I was a crazy person anymore. To be honest, I find this quite humorous. If they knew that I sold my dead wife's belongings because I saw my dead wife alive and then die again, they would think I was even crazier. Good thing crazy is easy to hide. It does not take a college degree to know children prefer bows and stickers.

12

I Only Wanted to See
(September 2031)

Once I gave my product the proper aesthetics, things moved along quickly. I made sale after sale. I moved out of my garage and into a small shop. I gathered a small team. I never revealed to the team the contents of my secret ingredient. The product has a long shelf-life, so I made it in large batches in my garage and then transported it to the shop where my employees baked with it. Just a couple drops of the stuff would last a day or two. A little goes a long way. Especially when poison is concerned.

My original team was made up of two boys and one girl. The boys' names were Gilbert Shepherd and Inglewood Sassafras. The girl's name was Layla Weedwacker. I said "were" about the boys' names because they have changed them since. They want nothing to do with me. I said "was" about the girl's name because she is dead.

The three employees were friends before they worked for me. At night, they put on a knife-throwing show, an odd kind of hobby that I allowed into the kitchen. Gilbert and Inglewood were the knife-throwers. They tied Layla to a wheel and spun her. Knife-throwing is one of the few sports where it is considered proper to miss on purpose.

That reminds me of an interesting aside. I used to think Inglewood walked on his tip-toes until one day I asked him about it. He took me aside. He put his hands on my shoulders in a pleading kind of way. My eyes went wide because I thought for one moment that he was going to kiss me.

"I don't walk on my tip-toes," he said. He put his hands down. He looked over his shoulders to make sure the others could not hear us.

I relaxed. "Yes, you do."

"No. I—"

I do not know why people reveal their secrets to me. I do not want my own secrets, let alone someone else's secrets. Maybe there is something in my eyes that calls to others deep in their being. Maybe they cannot help themselves.

"—I have hooves."

"..."

"..."

"Are you sure?" I knew it was a dumb question to ask. But I could not help myself, either. As soon as he told me, my goal was to get him to a state of mind where he would show me.

I like moments like that. When the illusions of life are shattered and all that matters is one thing. When he told me about his hooves, I forgot about my poison. I forgot about my dead wife. I forgot about breathing. I forgot about movies and books and commercials. I only wanted to see his hooves.

"Please don't tell anyone."

"I won't," I said, "but you have to show me. Or you're fired."

That did the trick.

<u>13</u>

Worse Things than Having Secrets
(August 2028)

A strange fact of life is that there are good secrets and bad secrets. The good secrets seem to occupy no space inside. They are easy to hold without pain. The bad secrets, though, are tiny little bombs with slow explosions and their explosions expand until fire makes its way up your esophagus and can be seen at the back of your throat. I thought I could hold onto other people's secrets. I learned that I can only hold onto them if they are the good kind.

The night my wife died I revealed to her a terrible secret. I had no intention of revealing this secret to her, but it took its toll on me. Over the course of a year, I talked to her less and less. Every time I opened my mouth, the fire at my throat tried to escape. I was compelled to hold it in. Maybe this is what dragons are: A representation of humans full of the world's bad kinds of secrets.

My wife became suspicious of me. I began to loath myself. I did not know the best way to say what I needed to say. It is a difficult thing, putting fire into words.

She went out with our friends while I stayed home, neurotic from this secret. I lost my job and laid on the couch. I watched television. She had coffee with co-workers. I could hardly move. If you think a day is heavy, wait until you have a terrible secret: Bombs and anvils, fire and stone.

My stomach knotted. I developed ulcers. There are few unseen, nonliving organisms in this world that can have physical effects on people. Secrets are one of them. Love is another.

Finally, I told her. I took her into the kitchen. I poured myself some water and drank it to put out the fire for a few minutes. She sat on one side of the table, and I sat on the other. I could hardly look at her.

"I know you've been having an affair," I said.

She was stunned. The anvil left me. The fire receded.

"How long have you known?" she asked.

"About a year."

We sat in silence for a long time. By then I was used to it. Used to the silence, I mean. She was just an amateur. She squirmed and resisted the pressure that comes with silence. A terminal patient resisting death, I thought. She stood, she grabbed her purse, walked out of the house, to her car, and drove away. She did not say a word. That was the night I got the call. That was the night she went to sleep.

I would endure the fire and the anvil and the silence and the ulcers to have her back. I was foolish to think I could gain that kind of peace without taking from someone else. There are worse things than having secrets.

<u>14</u>

Giant Wooden Blocks
(September 2031)

I went home from work one night to find the area around my house surrounded by police cars and fire trucks and ambulances. There were body bags and broken glass and yellow tape. Reporters and television news teams asked the police questions and were ignored. Cars were smashed down their centers with their fronts and backs sandwiched together, pointed toward the sky, as though only their middles were crushed by thin, long, metal pipes.

I pulled over and walked toward my house. A police detective stopped me.

"What happened?" I asked.

He ignored me.

"I live right there," I pointed at my house. "Can I get through or should I come back later?"

"You live *there*?" he asked.

"Yes."

"Come with me."

He took me aside, pulled out a notepad, and questioned me away from the reporters.

"Where were you about twenty minutes ago?"

"I was at work," I said.

"Are there others who can verify that you were there?"

"Yes." I told him to talk to Layla, Gilbert, and Inglewood.

After he wrote their names, he told me, "We don't know what happened. Our only witness is that kid," and he pointed at a boy about ten years old, "who says that giant wooden blocks and bars 'appeared' and 'fell from the sky' and they landed on people and cars and crushed them."

I looked around. "Where are the blocks?" I asked. He gave me a funny look. The kind of look you might give to a grown man who was duped by a ten-year-old.

"He says they disappeared." The detective looked upset. "It looks like something smashed a decent-sized hole in your house," he said, pointing to where my wife drove through the wall. "Sorry about that."

"That was already there," I said. "Can I go get something to eat to give you some space?"

He smiled. "We'll be in touch as we figure this thing out." He gave me his card.

I got some food and saw a movie. By the time I returned, everything was cleaned up. I went into my garage and heard squeaking noises. Some of my secret ingredient was spilled on the floor. I walked to the box of my product and mice ran away. A mouse chewed its way through a box and into one of the vials.

Mousetraps.

15

Maybe Three Feet
(September 2031)

I went to the patent office to check on the status of my submission. Inglewood was running the shop. He did not want to run the store without me there. After I told him Layla was working with him, he did not mind. Inglewood was head over hooves for her.

On the wall of the patent office lobby there was a list of famous patents and their creators. Each creator had a short biography: A spouse or two listed, maybe some children, a small list of their likes and dislikes. It is an amazing thing how much we know about the dead. If the dead knew what the living know about them, even death could not conceal their shame. They would dig themselves up to explain themselves.

Also, I do not understand intellectual property. It is one of the few properties that remain a part of a person after they die. Land and wealth, for example, are passed to the next generation. Book collections are sold or given away. Photographs are boxed in attics. Ideas are different, though. It is the things that people think that we publicly acknowledge to belong to the deceased. There are good objections to this claim. For example, family recipes appear to be ideas that are passed to others after death. However, it is one thing to have a family recipe and to pass it down through children and another thing to will an idea to someone as if it were their own. Now that I think about it, graves are another property that stay with a person in death. Actually, it is a person's property only in death. One does not really own a grave before one dies. Do they?

The patent office was deserted again. I walked to the man at the desk and asked about my application. He told me he would check. He stood and went to a computer at another desk. He opened a few drawers and typed on the computer. I had no idea what he was doing. He could have been conjuring demons with the blood of Aleister Crowley online for all I knew. I understand filing about as well as I understand intellectual property.

He returned and sat down at his desk.

"It's already taken," he said.

"Impossible," I said.

"Improbable," he corrected.

I hate the patent office.

"Your application has been rejected because the patent has already been filed. About twenty-three years ago."

"Who filed it?" I asked.

"Logan C. Bates."

"Is he still alive? Where does he live?"

"I can't tell you that."

Until that moment I never knew why I carried a water balloon with me wherever I went. I pulled it out of my backpack and threw it at the man as hard as I could. I hit him in the face. I was maybe three feet from him. He did not even know to try to dodge it. This is the beauty of a water balloon in a formal situation: No one expects it.

As the man either pretended to be unconscious on the ground or was actually unconscious on the ground, I looked at his computer.

Logan C. Bates.

Sixty-six years old.

Widower. No children.

Likes: Gold panning.

Dislikes: Car enthusiasts.

Current Location: Nome, Alaska.

16

May I?
(November 2031)

Hyo sent me a map detailing, as best as he could, the way to a small makeshift runway east of Nome. I had only been to Nome once before, back in September, when I first visited Logan at his aluminum shack inside the city limits. That was before the sanctions were placed. Things were different during my second trip to Alaska. There was a miserableness that followed me in the overcast sky. A hopelessness in every part of one great cloud. Alaska has a special silence about it. Hopelessness is a kind of silence.

Hyo's map was hand-drawn with red crayon on green construction paper. A series of smiley faces followed a trail in the wilderness from Nome. The runway was a thin line with a crude Russian flag above it. I assumed that was the way to go.

I walked through a meadow and along a creek. Round and smooth stones broke my steps with pleasant crackles. That is how I often feel, like I walk with pleasant steps under a sky of hopelessness.

When I arrived, two men were waiting next to a small propeller plane. They had rifles over their shoulders. They were joking with each other. People pick strange times to joke, just like they do to be polite.

The men did not point their rifles at me. But they were not laid back about my presence. One stood next to the plane while the other walked to me.

"May I?" he asked.

I did not know what that meant. Until that moment, I had never begun a conversation that way. I assumed he wanted to see my secret ingredient. I pulled a mason jar out of my backpack. The jar was filled with the product. Just a couple of drops lasts a day or two. That is, when you are baking with it. The man held the jar to the sun and looked through it. The liquid refracted the light: Liquid crystals, diamond poison.

The man made a motion and his partner jogged to us.

The closer the partner came, the more I realized he was just a kid, maybe twenty. The man handed the kid the mason jar. The kid opened it. He smelled it and studied it. He looked to the man. The kid smiled. Then the kid took the biggest drink of the stuff I had ever seen anyone take.

17

Slow and Heavy
(September 2031)

The first time I arrived in Nome I did not know what to expect. I thought maybe everyone lived in holes in the ground. Or wherever it is that gnomes live. I assumed it was Gnome, Alaska. Turns out the G is silent. Locals were all too happy to point this out to me.

Nome was like a town made of the large aluminum workshops in my dad's friends' backyards. It was a town of shacks. A place where the cultural center is connected to the post office and both are run by volunteers.

No one picked me up. No one in Alaska knew I was coming. Only one person in regular America knew I was leaving. My plan was to arrive at the house of Logan C. Bates and talk to him. I had no business reason for being in Nome. I needed to know if Logan had the same experiences that I had. It is a strange thing to lust after someone else's knowledge.

Logan's house was just another aluminum shack, one in the middle of a long row of other people's aluminum shacks. None of the neighbors had any idea who it was they were neighboring. I once thought my neighbor was an interesting character. He went around talking to himself. And not in a cute curmudgeon or genius eccentric kind of way, but in a real creepy, crazy, and hostile kind of way. But he was nothing compared to Logan C. Bates.

I walked up the few steps to Logan's front door. There was a note on the door.

Come in.

So I did.

I opened the door and saw a heavily bearded outdoorsman in his sixties. His feet were about six inches off the floor. A rope was around his neck.

The way he dangled reminded me of one of those giant clocks at science museums. The ones that keep time with a rod hanging from a wire. It knocks over blocks as the earth rotates: Slow and heavy.

18

Royalties
(November 2031)

After the kid took the drink, this is what happened:

The air took on the appearance of flowing glass. Cracks appeared in our dimension and spread. Chips of reality fell to the ground like broken pottery and revealed universes, stars, galaxies, obscurities, wonder. The sun flickered, a dying lamp, and the kid fell to the ground and grabbed his head and screamed. He split into infinite reflections of himself, from infrared to ultraviolet, stretching in a line across the horizon in opposite directions. His screams took on a digital and electric sound. He bled from his eyes and his ears.

There was a sudden force pulling me toward the kid. The trees and the waters were pulled toward him, too. The sun seemed to grow larger, as if it were pulled toward him. He was a human supernova. The man yelled something to the kid in Russian. The kid shook his head no with a sob. The man repeated himself. The kid did not say anything more. The kid then took his rifle, put it in his mouth, and pulled the trigger.

The trees, the waters, me, and the Russian man were thrown back as we were released from the kid's gravitational pull. The kid's body was on the ground in a pool of blood.

We stood and gathered ourselves. I walked to the kid's body. The eyes were still open. The mason jar was not broken and contained more than half of its contents.

"So," the man said, as if nothing had happened, "we have a deal?"

I was still looking at the kid's body. "OK," I said.

"Here," the man handed me some papers, "sign this for your royalties. You will receive a payment every month from our sales in Korea and in Georgia."

I looked at him. "Royalties?"

"Yes," he said. "We're not crooks. We pay you for your work. The worker is worthy of his wages."

I gave him the mason jar and the recipe for my secret ingredient for mass distribution.

"For my sake," I said, "I hope you're wrong."

19

A Man's Vapor
(September 2031)

In front of the hanged Logan there was a bedside table. A small vial with liquid in it. And a note.

The note read:

You don't remember the first time we met. I made sure it never happened in your current life. You haven't yet perfected the formula as I have. Mine is more specific. Mine can trans-place more than random memories. I can travel across time.

I'm not going to stop you. Soon you'll hear from the president. Sanctions will be placed.

My vision flashed. Voices spoke in my head.

{You already know what I'm going to do with this?}
{Yes. But that's not why I killed myself.}

My vision returned. The body of Logan C. Bates was gone. An empty rope hung from the ceiling.

"Tea?" a voice asked me.

I turned and saw Logan standing in front of me. He offered me a steaming mug. I looked at the vial on the table. It was empty.

"You already drank it," said Logan.

The lights in the house dimmed.

"No, I didn't."

"Well," said Logan, "maybe not *this* time. But you drink it once, you drink it always. You drank it the last time we had this conversation. And the time before that. You would have eventually."

The echoes of times and lives washed over me. The poison was in my system. One Logan returned to the noose. Another Logan appeared and vacuumed his carpet. Another looked out of his front window.

"Tea?" Logan offered again.

My head hurt. The pain was excruciating. I sat on his couch.

"I don't want you to make this deal with the Koreans and the Russians," said Logan.

"What deal?"

Logan smiled. "That's your next trip to Nome, isn't it? Well, I don't want you to do that. And I don't want you to unleash this on the world. You need to shut down your shop. I've already set in motion events that will make sure the government is involved in stopping you."

"You already know what I'm going to do with this?" I asked.

"Yes," said Logan. "But that's not why I killed myself."

{It's true what they say—}

"—a man's vapor is but a life."

I tried to stand to leave. I fell to my knees. My skull was about to split open. The claustrophobia of sickness pressed in. The smell of his house, the words he spoke, the anxiety that this feeling would never end, all caused an irrepressible and inescapable sickness in me.

"Don't worry," he said. "I'll release you."

The Logans disappeared. There was just the swinging body. There was just a man as a clock.

I had everything I needed. I did not want his knowledge anymore. Another man's knowledge can be frightening. I stood. I had a minor headache. I walked out of his house and made my way back home.

20

Where the Rabbit Waits
(October 2031/January 2027)

Two dresses, one pair of shoes, a photo frame, and her favorite book was what I could find at the thrift shops. These items were what I rounded up of my dead wife's belongings, the ones I traded for bows and stickers. Finding the items took a while.

I stood in my living room staring at them. I focused on memories of our time together. These were memories I usually tried not to think about. I do not know how memories of things that have happened can still cause unpleasantness. The truth is that I was afraid to remember them, as if not thinking about them might make them never have happened.

My wife's articles encircled me. This was modern voodoo, real magic. I was going to pull the rabbit out of the hat.

Man crumples and dies.

I put the poison to my lips. I closed my eyes. In the vial was not my original secret ingredient. If Logan could alter it, so could I. And I did. I altered it.

I took a drink. I felt nothing. When I opened my eyes, though, I was in a public restroom. It was instantaneous. I could not tell the poison had taken hold. It was a nice restroom. There were dark tiling flooring and marble counters. I walked to the sink, turned on the faucet, and rubbed water on my face.

I walked out of the restroom and saw I was in a restaurant. I scanned the room. There she was, at a small table for two, sitting alone, waiting. I did not bring her to me. I brought myself to her. I did not pull the rabbit out of the hat. I fell into the hat and wound up where the rabbit waits.

She looked at her menu and she smiled. It had been so long since I had seen her smile. Even before the car accident, it had been a while. I walked toward her.

A waiter cut me off. Then another. A stranger walked in front of me. More and more people got in my way. I put up my hands to call out her name. I hesitated when her attention was grabbed by someone else. An older man. His back was to me. Her smile widened at the sight of him. He walked up to her. They kissed. This was the man she was seeing while I had ulcers and secrets and fire. The man turned around and sat down. The man was Logan C. Bates: Gold Panner and Car Unenthusiast.

21

Scream Into the Pipes
(January 2027)

What was I supposed to do?

I did not want to confront her. I did not want to ruin anything—In a space time and cosmic sense, I mean. But an opportunity like this does not come often.

I could not decide to whom I wanted to speak, her or Logan. I had no sense of how much time I had before my secret ingredient brought me back. If it would bring me back at all, that is.

I decided, at the very least, I should warn her about the car accident. That was one thing I knew for certain I could do. She and Logan can live together if they want, but I thought I would at least hold the door open for her to live a little longer. That is what civilized people do for one another.

The path cleared. No one was in my way. I took a step forward. Logan looked away from her and right to me. He knew who I was. Even though I met him after he died, he definitely recognized me.

I stopped. He said something to her and got up. He pointed in another direction, she nodded, and continued looking at her menu. He walked toward me with a deter-mined look on his face. *Determined* is probably the best word

I can use to describe how he walked and how he looked while doing it.

I took a step back. I retreated into the bathroom. *Retreated* is probably the best word I can use to describe what it was that I did and how I felt about doing it.

The bathroom door opened, and Logan walked through. He walked straight to me and flattened me to the floor with one punch. He twisted my arm behind my back and lifted me. He rammed me into the toilet stall. He held my hair and submerged my head in the toilet water. He put his body weight on my back. I could not move. All I could do was scream into the pipes.

22

Truth to Fiction
(October 2031/February 2027/
March 2027/April 2027/etc.)

I stood in my house screaming. In an instant, I returned. My hair was wet, and my face and the front of my shirt were soaked with toilet water.

I was lost in a world of memory. I did not know how much of what I knew was true. Memories can lie. Memories can change. They flawlessly convert truth to fiction whether we want them to or not.

This was not my memory from which I returned. It was her memory. Was it a memory of what actually happened? Or was it a memory the way she remembered it, whether it was historically true or not? And how did Logan get there? Did I bring Logan with me? Had I altered the past or just visited it?

I was not going to wait to answer my questions. I had enough of my modified secret ingredient. I drank it and I thought about the unthinkable.

When I opened my eyes, I was outside a coffee house that my wife liked. It was daytime. She was drinking coffee and talking with Logan. They were holding hands. I blinked and another week passed. I was at her friend's house on a night she went over for dinner while I stayed home. They were all in the kitchen. Logan was with them.

In moments I passed through month after month, and it was Logan each time. She was with Logan everywhere she went. I knew she was having an affair, but seeing it after spending so long trying not to think about it shook me. I was furious. I decided to visit her one last time. In the blink of an eye and the notion of my will, I stood on the sidewalk and watched the street and waited for her car to come around the corner and crash into the building downtown.

<u>23</u>

Things We Do Not Witness
(August 2028)

It was about nine o'clock at night. I sat on the curb. The building my wife was going to crash into was a brick laundromat. I sat across the street from it, staring and waiting. The street was empty. There were no cars or people.

My neighbor's cat walked to me. The cat rubbed against my leg. I picked it up and we waited together.

The majority of our lives is made up of things we do not witness. I had not before seen my wife's car accident. But it impacted me far more than anything else. It brought about my loneliness. It brought about my secret ingredient. It brought about Logan and Nome and fury and rage and sorrow. And it was about to happen all over again. I had no intention, though, of trying to stop it.

In the distance, a pair of headlights turned down the road.

"This won't make you feel better," said Logan. He sat down next to me.

The car in the distance pulled to the side of the road. The passenger side door opened. A person stepped out.

"That's me," said Logan. "We had just been talking about you. She told me that you told her you knew she was seeing someone. I was worried you knew about us, but she said you didn't."

The passenger stepped away from the car and walked away. The car pulled back into the street. It drove toward us.

"Come on," said Logan. "Let's go."

"No," I said.

The car was about a half-mile away.

"Why did you do it?" I asked.

Six blocks.

Logan did not answer.

"You could have been anywhere and with anyone," I said. "I've seen what you can do. Why her?"

Four blocks.

"Because," he replied. Then he paused.

Two blocks.

"I don't have much time left," he continued. "I want to spend it with someone."

She stopped at a red light.

"But *why her*?" I asked.

"Because of you."

I didn't know what to say to that.

"I won't watch this," he said.

"Why not?" I asked.

He turned away. "I've seen it too many times."

The light turned green.

"Please," I said, "leave her alone."

"No. But you won't see me again."

Logan was gone.

Her tire popped. The car swerved. She put her hands up over her face. She crashed into the wall. The airbag did not deploy. I set the cat on the ground. The cat's ears bent back. The streetlights flickered. My wife was dead. I did not stay any longer.

24

Untrained in Fear
(December 2031)

I hesitate to call my second trip to Nome a success. But I accomplished the American dream there. In this sense, it could be called successful. I became very well off because of the deal and the subsequent underground business, what with all of the royalties.

The Russians were able to replicate my poison. In turn, they made sure it found its way to North Korea, Kazakhstan, Iran, Georgia, Turkey, Egypt, and Libya. My product fell into a lot of hands with a lot of intentions. And this is where it all went wrong.

I apologize. I should not write things like "it fell" or "it found its way." Words like that makes the action itself sound passive. The truth is that I put my product into the hands of uncivilized people. I stepped into the woods, I called to the creatures, I took a file, and I sharpened the fangs of beasts.

The first bombing still plays in my mind. There was amateur footage of it on the news the day it happened. The footage is still available in dark corners of the web. The bombing happened in Chicago.

I remember the video clearly. The video is of a group of kids. They were on a field trip at the Chicago Board of Trade Building. A parent was filming from the back of the group. The children and teachers were walking into the building.

The video shows the kids at the front of the line enter the building. Then a blast of flames shoots out into the street. The flames and the dust of shattered glass plumes. The person with the camera does not run into the flames to check on the children. This person is untrained in fear. The person with the camera runs away. Their identity was not released because of how they responded, so as to protect them. Being civilized is not always a matter of choice.

When I first watched the video, I had no idea my secret ingredient had anything to do with the event. Other people did, though. There were more eyes on me than I realized.

After the video played on the news, my phone rang. I answered it.

"Are you watching the news?" the voice asked me.

"Yes," I said.

"We know about the deal you made with the Russians," the voice said.

"So do all of North Korea, Iran, and Egypt. Word moves slowly for the civilized in the Information Age."

"Do you know who this is?" the voice asked.

"No."

"This is the president of the United States. The bombing on the news is your fault."

"How's that?"

"You don't know how?" he asked. He scoffed. "Word moves even slower for the uncivilized."

The president then explained to me how I single-handedly committed one of the greatest atrocities of our time.

25

Twice Now
(October 2031)

I went to my office and sat at my desk. I did nothing for the rest of the night. I thought I would catch up on some business since I was away for a few days in Alaska. I could not concentrate on work.

A knock on my door woke me. At the door was the detective from the mousetrap case. It was morning.

"Can I come in?"

"Yes," I said.

He stepped through the door. He did not sit.

"Do you remember me?" he asked.

"Yes."

"There was an incident last night," he said.

"What happened?"

"It appears that your employees Gilbert and Inglewood murdered Layla. They were practicing their knife-throwing act. They didn't miss. We suspect murder because it wasn't only one knife. When we arrived, there were close to fifteen knives stuck in her. After they called 911, they called me. I spoke with them after talking to you about the crushed vehicles. To verify that you were indeed working during that time. I told them if anything strange happened to give me a call."

"I don't understand why they called you."

"Because," said the detective, "according to them, something strange happened. I need you to come with me to the station to talk to them."

We walked to his car. I got in the back. He pulled into the street and drove.

"There have been two incidents of a strange and sudden appearance and disappearance that somehow have you in them. First the 'giant wooden blocks' that kid saw and now this."

"What do they say happened?"

"They say that they drank something you make but you won't tell them what it is, and that knife-throwers appeared out of nowhere, threw a bunch of knives at Layla, and then disappeared."

I could not tell if he believed them or not.

"Take me to my house first," I said, "I think I can straighten this out."

He pulled into my driveway. We went into my garage. I opened a safe and took out all of the vials that were in it. This was the entire stash of the old secret ingredient, not the modified product. I gave them all to him.

"What's this?" he asked.

"This is my secret ingredient. Be careful. I've twice now seen my dead wife alive and then die again."

I pulled out my phone.

"Who are you calling?" the detective asked.

"A couple lawyers. I want them to meet us at the station."

26

Silent Chaos
(October 2031)

At the police station, in front of armed guards, a team of detectives, and an assembly of lawyers, I demonstrated my secret ingredient in action. I was the first to drink it. This was the stuff I used at my store, not my improved and amended secret ingredient. I was not sure what was coming. The lights flickered. The guards tensed. My wife appeared.

"What's going on?" she asked me. The guards raised their weapons at her.

"I'm showing them what I can do," I said.

"Be careful," she said. "You might never see me again."

"I don't think I will," I said.

She looked at the police and lawyers in the room: Uniforms and ties, guns and books.

"Are they going to lock you away?" she asked.

"I don't know," I said.

She smiled and put her hand on my face. The lights flickered. Then she was gone. A withered whisper in a room of silent chaos.

The guards and detectives and lawyers were baffled. They thought I was pulling something over on them. I offered a vial to anyone who wanted to try some.

27

When Someone Wants It
(October 2031)

There was no law against what I had done. The lawyers said the police had no right to hold me. There was no precedent, unlike *I Love Lucy*. The police came to my house and seized what was in my garage, but they could not keep me from making more. That was the beginning of placing sanctions on my business. They were going to use the law any way they could to keep me from doing what I do best, and sanctions were all they had in the meantime.

Word escaped quickly. Professors from universities wanted to buy some from me. For a brief couple of days, I sold some to them, which is one of the ways the product was released in America. Then pharmaceutical companies contacted me. The sanctions were placed before I gave them my answer. That is how quickly it happened.

The government wanted some. I told them no. A process immediately began to seize every last drop of poison. It is funny how quickly bureaucracy can work when someone wants it to work. They forbade me from ever making it again. They had no way of enforcing me making it again, however. I could go to any department store and get the equipment to make it for less than the cost of a fine meal.

Since my situation was unprecedented, they decided to place sanctions solely on my business. They seized all of my equipment at work. They thought I could only make the stuff using heavy machinery. The only part of my work that was left was my office. Well, that and the asbestos.

My business was profitable in its short life. Even though I had no employees and no equipment after the sanctions were finalized, I still went to work for the next month. I could afford to be at work. Plus, I had nothing better to do. In November was when I received the call from Hyo.

28

The Second Time
(December 2031)

I did not believe the president at first when he explained what his intelligence revealed: That I was responsible for the first bombing. But then another bombing was played on a different news channel. Then another. And another. All of the clips were consistent in a disturbing way. They all had children in them.

There is a reason all the clips had children. The older a person becomes, the harder it is to determine what effect my secret ingredient will bring about for the user. The opposite is also true. The younger a person is, the easier it is to determine what will happen when they take my poison. The version of my secret ingredient that was released was the basic version, not my updated version I learned after meeting Logan in Alaska. That is a secret I kept to myself.

Military groups in North Africa and West Asia were kidnapping children and forcing them to watch videos of suicide bombers. The children were then sent to the U.S. with a vial of my poison. The children would drink it, then suicide bombers would appear and detonate.

That military groups did this to children became a publicly well-known fact. Videos of the camps were posted

online and through news agencies. The videos are haunting:
Hoards of children sitting in dark dens and watching grue-
some videos projected on a wall.

My name was everywhere. I was not about to be handed
a Nobel prize. Thus, the president called me. He wanted me
in hiding.

"We're sending you away for good," said the president.

"Where?" I asked.

"We're sending you back to Nome. It'll be easier the
second time," he said.

When he said that, I realized that they did not know
about my first visit.

"And," he said, "we have a new name ready for you."

"I don't need a new name," I said.

"Your new name," he said, "is Logan."

"Logan?"

"That's right," he said. "Logan C. Bates. There was a man
there by that name who just committed suicide. It has a nice
ring to it, though. Why don't you take up some gold panning?
Or maybe cars?"

"Yes," I said. "Some gold panning maybe. I've never been
much interested in cars."

<u>29</u>

A Kind of Poison
(July 2032)

That is why Logan wanted to be with her, why he wanted to spend what time he had left with her. She knew who Logan really was. She knew Logan needed her more than I did.

I am in Nome now. I live in an aluminum shack. It is one aluminum shack among many.

I visit her often by using my modified secret ingredient that no one knows exists. She smiles a lot more than I remember. She calls me Logan. She laughs when she does it.

I perfected my secret ingredient. I can slip in and out of time and memories. As long as I do not return to the lower states apart from using my secret ingredient, no one will bother me.

I go to her memories, and I see her more than I spend time here, in the present. I do not know if this way of living is good or bad. I know I want to live the rest of my days in peace. I started to grow a beard. Beards seem peaceful.

She knows that Logan comes and sees her. She does not know there is a noose in my room. It is a noose I will have to use when some lost man visits Nome. I will leave a note on the door for when he knocks and wants to know how I have a patent to his secret ingredient.

A noose is a kind of poison. It is a poison both for the civilized and for the uncivilized. But it is a poison that I do not want to think about just yet.

END